JOURNEY TO ERIDANUS

TZANGEL
Journey to Eridanus

For more information or to book an event, contact:
Tzangel@gmail.com

Book design by TZANGEL (aka Bonita Corbett)
Cover design by TZANGEL (aka Bonita Corbett)

Published by Spines
ISBN: 979-8-89569-204-2
First Edition: March 2024

JOURNEY TO ERIDANUS

THE SEQUEL TO THE SHADOWY SECRETS

TZANGEL

DEDICATION

To the star seeds awakening in us all,
And to those who heed the cosmic call,
This journey is dedicated, with love so true,
May it awaken the light within you.

ACKNOWLEDGMENT

To My Beloved Readers,

I stand here once more, pen in hand, heart brimming with gratitude. As I embark on the next chapter of this magickal journey, I am reminded of the unwavering support that has carried me thus far.

My Mom, the beacon of strength and grace, your unwavering belief in my dreams continues to fuel my spirit. You taught me resilience, and for that, I am forever indebted.

Anthony, my King, and Soulmate, your patience during the creative storms is my anchor. Through ups and downs, you remain my unwavering lighthouse, guiding me home.

My family, you've weathered my wild ideas, celebrated my victories, and held me close during the storms. Your love is the bedrock upon which my stories thrive.

Summer & Jessica, my ethereal muses, your laughter and wonder breathe life into Saturn Eridanus. You are the magick woven into every word.

Ashley, Laura, and Patricia, my sisters from other mothers, your wisdom and unwavering friendship has been my sanctuary. You've read my drafts, listened to my midnight rants, and loved me fiercely. The Goddess truly blessed me with your presence.

And to **everyone else**, those unseen stars who whispered encouragement shared their light, and believed in my journey—I feel your vibrations. Together, we dance on the same frequency, weaving a tapestry of connection and inspiration.

Lastly, to the **Goddess**, the cosmic weaver of destinies, I bow in reverence. Your abundance flows through my veins, and I send it forth, multiplied, to touch every reader's heart.

Thank you, dear readers, for joining me on this enchanting voyage. May our paths continue to intersect, and may the magick endure.

With love and ink-stained blessings,
TZANGEL

PREFACE

In the vast expanse of the cosmos, where stars shimmer like promises and galaxies twirl in eternal dances, a realm of magick and mystery intertwines—an ancient domain where time weaves destiny's tapestry. Welcome to the journey to Eridanus.

In the serene silence before a transformative journey, Saturn Eridanus and Miles Nightshade stood at the edge of the unknown, their destinies intertwined with the cosmos. The culmination of 'The Shadowy Secrets' was not an end but the beginning of an adventure poised to defy time and fate. With Saturn's celestial lineage and Miles as her unwavering guardian and companion, they embarked on a quest for truths concealed by the pages of history—where the mysteries of the Conclave of Shadows endangered their unborn daughter, a beacon of their heritage.

Their mission, forged from love, strength, and an insatiable thirst for knowledge was as daring as it was dangerous. Together, they sought to unravel the Conclave's ancient vendetta against Saturn's ancestors—animosity now endangering their infant, a symbol of hope and legacy.

As they prepared for departure, the resonance of their alliance was palpable, a formidable power akin to enchantment. The spell they wove, blending ancient rites with Miles's time manipulation illuminated their path through uncertainty. Their preparations—herbs, crystals, and talismans—reflected resolve and the interplay of destiny and autonomy.

In the concealed fire ring amidst Nightshade Mansion's lush depths, Saturn and Miles stood as one. The magick under the moon's watchful eye, amidst forest spirits heralded more than a journey—it proclaimed solidarity, kinship, and defiance against the encroaching darkness.

When they crossed the portal, they carried an aspiration to illuminate the past and a vision for a future where light triumphs.

"Journey to Eridanus" unfolds as a tale of love, courage, and relentless pursuit of truth. It spans time's fabric, testing protagonists' grit, faith, and allegiance. As they navigate history's waters, they carve a path toward enlightenment.

This preface beckons readers into an epic beyond time and space—a voyage of cosmic mysteries and the human spirit. Join Saturn and Miles in their crusade for family, legacy, and existence.

PROLOGUE

In the ethereal silence that blankets the cosmos, where stars whisper secrets to the void, Saturn Eridanus and Miles Nightshade embarked on a voyage that would etch their names across the annals of time. With hearts fortified by a shared resolve, they ventured beyond the veil of reality, guided by ancient time travel and Miles' mastery over the temporal realm. Their destination was the the constellation of Eridanus, a celestial haven shrouded in mystery and lore, heralded as Saturn's ancestral realm. It was here, amidst the stars that bore her name, that they sought to unravel the tangled threads of her lineage and confront the obscured truths of a past long veiled.

Armed with the knowledge that their journey would pierce the heart of the unknown, Saturn and Miles wove through the tapestry of the cosmos, their path illuminated by the arcane energies of the spell. The universe, vast and unbounded, stretched out before them, a canvas of infinite possibilities. They encountered realms where the fabric of reality bent in impossible ways, nebulae that painted the darkness with vibrant hues, and celestial bodies that sang in harmonies understood only by the cosmos itself.

With each discovery, their journey deepened, not just in distance but in meaning. The peril they faced was not merely physical but existential as they navigated through star systems that tested their resolve and planets that challenged their understanding of life and existence. Encounters with beings of light and energy, entities that defied the laws of physics, and civilizations built on the foundations of knowledge lost to their world offered glimpses into the vast tapestry of cosmic life. These experiences, both wondrous and harrowing, were markers of their passage, each one a step closer to the secrets that Saturn yearned to uncover.

Yet, it was the promise of discovery, the burning desire to protect their future, and the legacy that would follow that propelled them forward. Saturn and Miles were not merely explorers but guardians of a new era, seeking the wisdom needed to safeguard their unborn daughter. This child, a symbol of hope and a bridge between the past and the future was the silent beacon that guided their way through the darkest reaches of space.

Their love, a force as potent as any magick, bound them together in the face of the unknown. It was a testament to their strength and dedication, a bond that transcended the dimensions of time and space. Together, they faced the mysteries of the cosmos, their spirits intertwined in a dance as ancient as the stars themselves.

As they drew nearer to the heart of Eridanus, the anticipation of what lay ahead quickened their pulse. The constellation, with its myriad of secrets and ancient lore, beckoned with a call as old as time itself. Here, in the cradle of Saturn's origins lay the answers to questions that had haunted her since the beginning of their odyssey. The truths hidden within the constellation of Eridanus held the key to understanding the vendetta of the Conclave of Shadows, the mysteries of her lineage, and the destiny that awaited their family.

This prologue, a gateway to their journey, sets the stage for an epic tale of discovery, courage, and the indomitable spirit of two souls bound by love and destiny. As Saturn and Miles navigate the cosmic sea, their story unfolds—a narrative woven from the fabric of the stars, a saga of enlightenment, and a testament to the power of unity in the face of the vast, uncharted cosmos.

CHAPTER 1

ECHOES OF ERIDANUS: EMBRACING DESTINY

Colors swirled around us, a breathtaking display of cosmic energy. Stars streaked past like shooting stars, their brilliance lighting our path as we ventured deeper into the past. With each passing moment, the fabric of reality shifted and bent, revealing glimpses of history long forgotten. Finally, we arrived in the enchanting realm of Eridanus, a place that defied imagination.

As Miles and I, two intrepid explorers, delved further into the universe, the stars seemed to draw us in like a celestial magnet. Each twinkling light beckoned us closer, promising untold adventures and mysteries waiting to be unraveled. The entire universe lay bare before us, inviting exploration of its boundless wonders.

Among the myriad stars, the graceful form of the

Eridanus constellation revealed itself. Its shimmering curves danced across the velvet sky, resembling a river of light flowing through the cosmos. We were spellbound by its beauty, feeling a sense of awe wash over us as we traced its celestial path, each moment revealing a new facet of its enchantment.

Eridanus, one of the five equatorial constellations, stretched out like a vast playground of stars. Its sprawling expanse covered an impressive 1138 square degrees, promising endless discoveries to those who dared to venture within its boundaries. At its forefront gleamed Achernar, the brightest star in the constellation, guiding us with its radiant glow like a beacon in the night. This constellation, named after the mythical river in Greek mythology, is a symbol of the cosmic journey we are about to embark on.

As we marveled at the wonders of Eridanus, our gaze was drawn to other notable stars dotting the cosmic canvas. Cursa, a majestic white giant, stood out with its luminous brilliance, while Acamar nestled among the stellar lineup, adding its celestial sparkle to the scene. Epsilon Eridani, with its confirmed exoplanet, served as a reminder of the countless worlds that existed beyond our own.

But Eridanus held more than just stars; it was a realm of mystery and intrigue, where deep sky objects beckoned with enigmatic allure. The Eridanus Super void, a vast emptiness stretching across the cosmic landscape, hinted at secrets waiting to be uncovered. The Witch Head Nebula, illuminated by neighboring Rigel, cast a haunting glow upon the celestial stage, captivating us with its ethereal beauty. These are just a few of the many wonders that await us in this cosmic realm.

The moment we stepped into Eridanus, it was as if the universe itself had enveloped us in its embrace. The forests around me were alive, a vibrant testament to the endless wonders the cosmos holds. The air buzzed with an energy that felt almost tangible, vibrating with the universe's rhythm, as if each breath carried the whispers of the cosmos directly to my soul. The ground beneath our feet seemed to pulse with the heartbeat of the universe, reminding us of its vastness and vitality.

Beneath the starlit canopy of Eridanus, the enchanted forest revealed its ancient and profound secrets. The magick-laden air brought the scent of night flowers to my senses, their glowing petals casting the undergrowth in ethereal shades of silver and blue. It was a realm where time stood still, a sanctuary bridging the realms, filled with the murmurs of ancient wisdom. The trees, tall and majestic, seemed to whisper secrets to each other, their branches reaching out like arms to welcome us into their realm.

Hand in hand with Miles, we ventured deeper into this enchanting realm, our path illuminated by the soft, ethereal glow of bioluminescent fungi. The forest's symphony

—a harmonious blend of the mysterious and the unknown —whispered of hidden creatures and promised untold adventures. 'Do you feel it, Miles?' I found myself whispering in breathless wonder, my senses overwhelmed by the sheer beauty and magick that enveloped us. 'The magick here... it's unlike anything we've ever experienced.'

Miles, his gaze lost to the horizon where the forest opened to rolling hills bathed in moonlight, nodded. "It's as if the air itself breathes stories, ancient tales, and wisdom with every breath we take."

Surrounded by Eridanus's splendor, Miles and I were awestruck. Here, reality and fantasy merged, and the universe's mysteries were laid bare for those brave enough to listen. Looking up at the constellation that marked this magickal realm, I knew our journey was far from over. It was a beginning, a promise of battles to be fought and secrets to uncover, all in the name of protecting this magickal world that, for a brief moment, we could call home. A home that had captured our hearts and ignited a fire within us.

Our exploration led us to a clearing where the remnants of a once-majestic temple stood. At its core was a crystal obelisk pulsating with a gentle, beckoning light. As I reached out to touch it, the past of Eridanus unfurled before my eyes—a beacon of light and magick, once harmoniously inhabited by a myriad of beings, until the encroaching darkness of the Conclave threatened this realm.

Stepping back, a resolve solidified within me. 'The Conclave has been a blight upon the cosmos for too long,' I declared. 'We must protect Eridanus.'

In that breathtaking moment, a surge of recognition washed over me like a gentle breeze, carrying whispers of memories long forgotten. 'Mom? Dad?' I called out, my voice quivering with anticipation as figures radiant with light drew near. Willow, her luminous aura enveloping her, and Sebastian, standing tall with a commanding yet comforting presence, stood before me—the parents I had never known, their untimely departure leaving me to navigate life's labyrinth without their guidance. But now, in this realm, their presence was palpable, their guidance a beacon in the darkness.

Willow, resembling a celestial goddess, emanated an aura of timeless elegance that seemed to reflect my essence. Her flowing chestnut-brown locks cascaded like liquid moonlight, dancing with the wind's gentle caress, each strand whispering secrets to the universe. Her face, perfectly rounded, framed by high cheekbones, exuded a natural radiance akin to the warmth of sun-kissed sands, yielding softly to the touch. Her lips curved delicately, hinting at unspoken tales, while her eyes, a mesmerizing fusion of rich brown and verdant green, held within them entire galaxies of emotion and wisdom.

Despite her petite stature of 5'4", Willow possessed a commanding presence that captivated all who beheld her. With each graceful movement, she seemed to glide effortlessly, her steps imbued with the fluidity of a seasoned dancer. Whether in a bustling ballroom or a serene garden, she wore sophistication like a second skin, causing the very air to shimmer with anticipation. As she drew closer, her gaze brimmed with maternal warmth, enveloping me in a comforting embrace that spoke of unconditional love.

Sebastian, towering at 6 feet 4 inches, exuded an aura of strength and grace that commanded attention from the moment he entered the room. His broad shoulders tapered down to a trim waist, a harmonious blend of athleticism and elegance that hinted at a life well-lived. His piercing icy blue eyes, reminiscent of glacial pools reflecting the Nordic sky, held depths of wisdom and secrets yet untold. His chiseled jawline, softened by a hint of vulnerability, spoke of resilience tempered with kindness, while his sun-kissed strands of hair fell in artful disarray, framing his features like a halo of warmth and light.

His smile, though rare, possessed a devastating charm that could brighten even the darkest of days, illuminating the room like the first rays of dawn breaking through storm clouds. And when he spoke, his voice, deep and resonant with a hint of gravel, carried an authority tempered by a gentle tenderness that drew me in like a moth to a flame. As he drew nearer, his gaze softened with paternal warmth, filling the void in my heart with a sense of belonging that I had long yearned for.

The moment our hands met, a surge of energy passed

between us—a connection that defied time and space. Tears welled in my eyes as the reality of touching, seeing, and feeling my parents overwhelmed me. "This moment, I've longed for it," I confessed, my voice choked with emotion. "I've missed you both so much."

"We've been watching over you, Saturn," Willow whispered, her voice a soft melody in the moonlit clearing, as she reached out to wipe away my tears. "Every step, every challenge—we've been there."

Her words enveloped me like a warm blanket, grounding me in the midst of overwhelming emotions. But then, like a gentle breeze carrying a secret whisper, she added, "And we, along with your ancestors whom you will soon meet; sent you Laila; a guardian angel to watch over and protect you."

The mention of Laila sparked a surge of excitement within me, dispelling the heaviness in my heart. "Yes! Yes, I know; she told me at my wedding reception," I exclaimed, my voice filled with uncontainable enthusiasm. "She's my best friend, and I love her; thank you for sending her to me."

Willow's gaze met mine, her eyes shimmering with understanding and warmth. With a gentle squeeze of my hands, she conveyed more than words ever could. It was a silent acknowledgment, a shared moment of gratitude and love that transcended the bounds of spoken language.

In that fleeting instant, amidst the cosmic expanse of

Eridanus, I felt a profound connection—not only to my celestial guardians but also to the earthly bonds that tethered me to this realm. And as Willow whispered, "You're welcome, my sweet girl," a soft smile gracing her lips, I knew that in this enchanted place surrounded by love and light, anything was possible.

"We are always with you, Saturn. Always," Willow and Sebastian assured, their embrace enveloping us in the warmth that felt like home.

Shifting gears in the conversation, Willow spoke, her voice soft yet imbued with a profound sense of strength. "Saturn, Miles," she began, her words carrying a weight of anticipation. "We've been expecting you; we've foreseen this."

Sebastian nodded in agreement, a mischievous twinkle in his eye. "Welcome to Eridanus. You're in for quite the adventure."

I couldn't help but grin at his words. "Well, we live for adventure."

Willow laughed, a melodic sound that echoed through the clearing. "That you do, my dear. But remember, not all adventures are without peril. You must tread carefully, for the path ahead is fraught with danger."

Miles squeezed my hand reassuringly, glancing over at my parents respectfully, and said, "Don't worry. We'll be careful. I'm not going to let anything happen to Saturn or our little girl."

Willow and Sebastian, responding with looks as if they

already knew about the baby, hugged and squeezed me and Miles, saying, "We are quite aware of the little one growing inside your belly; star seeds choose their path and their parents. We are beyond happy!" Willow, beaming at Sebastian, says, we're so excited to be grandparents!"

Willow's smile softened; her eyes filled with motherly affection. "While this is extremely awesome news, and I do know you will be careful, I can't help but worry. You're my daughter," and putting her hand on my belly, says, "and you're carrying our granddaughter after all."

I felt a lump form in my throat at her words. Despite everything, despite the dangers that lay ahead, I knew that Willow and Sebastian would always be there for us, watching over us with love and protection.

As we parted from their embrace, I knew that no matter what lay ahead, I carried within me the light of the cosmos, the love of my parents, and the strength of my bond with Miles. Together, we would face the future, guided by the stars and the eternal light that binds us all, ready to defend our world and ensure a brighter future for our unborn child.

The following day, we venture out and gravitate towards what turns out to be the Sanctuary, similar to what we call on earth a family room. I giggle to myself; Miles looks over at me with a grin as if hearing my thoughts. As we walk into the heart of the ancient Sanctuary, Miles and I find ourselves in a room bathed in ethereal luminescence. Crystals adorn the walls, casting prismatic hues across every surface, their elongated, striated forms standing like sentinels guarding secrets from a lost land. As we gaze upon them, I feel a connection stirring within me, as if the energy spiraling upward from the crystals is reaching out to touch our souls, linking us to the ancient ancestors who once communed with the stars.

At the heart of the ancient Sanctuary stands the enigmatic Celestial Shard, also revered as the Genesis Prism. Its cylindrical silhouette radiates with a dormant force, whispering secrets of the bygone Eridanian era. This civilization harnessed the Shard's dual essence, a combination of creation and destruction, to forge empires and unravel the very fabric of reality. The paradox of creation and destruction is intricately woven into its crystalline structure, a legacy of unparalleled might and wisdom that resonates across the eons.

As we move through the chamber, the walls shimmer with intricate patterns—a fusion of glyphs and geometries that whisper tales of healing waters, levitating temples and beings who effortlessly bridge realms, ethereal creatures with wings of light and bodies of stardust. The room resonates with their collective memories, enveloping us in a symphony of light and sound that seems to transcend time itself.

Sunlight filters through the crystal-studded windows, refracting into rainbows that dance upon the floor, while the air itself seems to hold whispers of ancient chants, forgotten spells, and the laughter of beings long gone, a symphony of sound that tells the story of a world lost to time. The crystals amplify this celestial chorus, inviting us to remember our cosmic origins and embrace the magick that pulses through our veins.

In one corner of the chamber, a shallow pool shimmers—a reflection of Eridanus's oceans. Here, one can immerse oneself, allowing the vibrations of the crystals to cleanse their spirit and transport them to distant realms, realms of floating islands, sentient forests, and starlit caves. As Miles and I float in its embrace, visions of lush forests, crystal cities, and gentle beings wash over us, bridging the gap between past and present.

Along the ceiling, Atlantean crystals hang suspended by invisible threads, pulsing with encoded knowledge and waiting for seekers to unlock their secrets. As we marvel at their luminescence, I can't help but wonder what mysteries lay hidden within their multifaceted depths, whether they hold the blueprints for advanced technologies or encode the very fabric of existence itself.

At the far end of the room, a crystal archway beckons, its shimmering form offering passage between dimensions. With each step closer, I feel the veils between past, present, and future blur, as if time itself is bending to accommodate our journey. It's our way back home, I think to myself, knowing that when we depart, we will carry with us the whispers of Eridanus's waves and the fiery echoes of Atlantis, the remnants of a lost civilization that still resonate within us, their gifts woven into the very fabric of our being.

After walking through the large room, Miles and I venture into the enchanted forests of Eridanus, where every tree seems to pulse with life. Colors explode around us, painting the world in hues of emerald and gold. magickal creatures flit through the foliage, their iridescent wings shimmering in the sunlight.

Returning to the Sanctuary, we find ourselves before Willow and Sebastian, our beloved grandparents, who await us with open arms. The news of their grandchild, our child, sparks a celebration, a moment of joy amidst the brewing storm.

Together, Miles and I walk a small distance from the Sanctuary to a clearing where the ancestors await. We are met with a sight that takes our breath away. Their ethereal forms glow with inner light, each one a beacon of wisdom and strength. As we approach, I feel a surge of reverence and awe wash over me.

Engaging in conversation with each ancestor, I listen intently as they share tales of their lives and experiences. Aurora, her golden gown shimmering in the sunlight, speaks of courage and leadership. Orion, his eyes sparkling with ancient wisdom, imparts lessons of knowledge and perseverance. Their words, like a warm embrace, fill me with a sense of connection and belonging, making me feel a part of their world.

The magickal luncheon with the ancestors is a feast for

the senses, as ethereal delights fill the air with tantalizing aromas and flavors. We sit together, sharing stories and laughter as we savor the moment. The table is adorned with dishes of ambrosial nectar, golden fruits that burst with celestial sweetness, and delicate pastries that melt in our mouths, leaving a trail of stardust on our tongues.

With each blessing and word of guidance from the ancestors, I feel a surge of clarity and purpose wash over me. Their wisdom, like a beacon in the night, illuminates the path ahead, instilling in me a deep sense of confidence and empowerment. I am reminded that I am not alone in this journey and that I carry the strength and wisdom of generations past within me.

As the afternoon sun begins to wane, we engage in activities that deepen our connection to the magick of Eridanus. We practice light weaving, a form of magick that allows us to shape and manipulate light, and stargazing, where we learn to read the constellations and understand their celestial messages. These activities fill our hearts with wonder, reminding us of the infinite possibilities that lie within our grasp.

The evening brings with it a sense of contentment and fulfillment as we gather around the dinner table with Willow and Sebastian. Sharing tales of our adventures and revelations, we laugh and reminisce late into the night.

Willow, her eyes reflecting the firelight, speaks of the importance of family and the strength it provides. "In times of darkness, our bond is the beacon that will guide you through. You, Saturn, and you, Miles, carry not just the hope of our lineage but the future of all realms within you."

Sebastian adds his voice firm, "And we will stand with you, against the Conclave or any who dare threaten our world. Together, we are a force that no darkness can overshadow."

As the night wears on, the conversation turns to strategies and alliances. "We need to gather allies, those who remember Eridanus and those willing to stand against the Conclave," I suggest, my mind already running through potential contacts and old friends who could lend their strength. The Conclave, a powerful and oppressive force, has been a thorn in our side for centuries, and it's time we took a stand.

I nod in agreement. "And we'll need to train, to harness the magick of Eridanus and the wisdom of our ancestors. There's so much we can learn from this place, from its history and its people."

Plans are made, and vows are renewed under the starlit sky, our family's determination shining as brightly as the constellations above. We speak of journeys to distant realms, of messages to be sent through the cosmic web, a vast and intricate network that spans across the universe, and of ancient artifacts that hold the key to unlocking powers long forgotten.

In the warm glow of family and love, I feel a profound sense of gratitude wash over me. No matter what challenges lay ahead, I know that we will face them together, supported by the unwavering love of those closest to us. Our ancestors, their spirits ever-present, guide us with their wisdom and strength, their voices echoing in our hearts.

As the day starts to take its toll on me, leaving me extremely exhausted, Miles and I retreat to our chambers, our hearts swelled with the richness of the day's experiences.

The first blush of dawn tiptoes through the curtains, coaxing me gently from my slumber. With a yawn and a stretch, I welcome another day in the enchanting realm of Eridanus. Emerging into the light-filled chambers, we find Willow and Sebastian already awake, their faces aglow with excitement as they greet us for breakfast. The air is thick with anticipation, buzzing around us like a swarm of eager fireflies as we discuss the day ahead. Our minds are already wandering to the mysteries waiting to be unraveled, the secrets of Eridanus that hold the key to our family's destiny.

With steaming cups of morning brew in hand, we embark on a journey through Saturn's lineage, a lineage steeped in power and mystery, each tale a thread weaving together the tapestry of her ancestry. Eridanus and Atlantis, the two realms that birthed our family, unfurl before us like ancient scrolls, their secrets whispered on the breeze, and we listen with rapt attention as the stories unfold. The connection between the family and the pulsing heart of Eridanus becomes more precise with each passing moment, like pieces of a cosmic puzzle slotting into place.

The 'ancient of ancient' Eridanus Book of Shadows, a tome as old as time itself, is impressive and beckons from its resting place. Its weathered pages whisper secrets known only to those who dare seek them. Filled with spells, rituals, and the forgotten history of our realm, we pore over its contents, each word a spark igniting our imaginations. Willow and Sebastian's insights add fuel to the fire, igniting lively debates and theories that dance like will-o'-the-wisps in the air around us.

Noontime finds us gathered with the ancestors, feasting on a banquet of ethereal delights, each dish a masterpiece of flavor and texture that seems to dance on our tongues with every bite. The flavors are like nothing I have ever tasted, each morsel a tantalizing tease of otherworldly cuisine. Under the watchful gaze of our forebears, we delve into the elemental arts, honing our skills with the precision of master artisans. The air crackles with energy as we weave spells, our voices rising in harmony with the rustling leaves and murmuring streams of Eridanus.

Exploration beckons us into the depths of the enchanted woods, a place where time stands still and magick is palpable, where secrets lay hidden beneath every leaf and stone. We hunt for treasures and artifacts that whisper tales of Saturn's lineage, each discovery a triumph in our quest for knowledge and understanding.

As the golden light of evening bathes the world in its

soft embrace, we gather around the hearth with our family, the crackling fire casting a warm glow upon our faces. Tales of Saturn's ancestors, their legendary exploits of bravery, wisdom, and sacrifice, dance in the flickering shadows, their stories painting a vivid picture of courage and resilience. With hearts full to bursting, we retreat to our chambers, the echoes of laughter and reflection trailing behind us like stardust.

CHAPTER 2
THE QUEST BEGINS

As the first light of dawn paints the skies of Eridanus in hues of hope and urgency, Miles and I find ourselves immersed in the ancient tome laid out before us. Our breakfast lies forgotten, abandoned in the wake of revelations unfolding within the pages. The history of the Conclave of Shadows, tracing back to the star of Arcturus, unveils more than a mere vendetta; it lays bare the map of the cosmic war, a battle for the very essence of existence, looming on our horizon.

The tome itself, a relic of the Eridanus Coven's vast library, seems to pulsate with the energy of generations past. Its leather-bound cover, weathered and worn, bears the marks of countless hands that have turned its pages. Each page whispers secrets of epochs gone by; its words are alive with the wisdom of those who have come before us. This library, a labyrinth of knowledge nestled within the heart of Eridanus, stands as a testament to the enduring pursuit of enlightenment. Its guardian, the venerable Thalios, awaits us, his presence as ancient as the stars themselves.

Thalios, a sage whose existence spans epochs, stands before us like a pillar of wisdom amidst the boundless expanse of knowledge. His form, cloaked in robes spun from threads of time, exudes an aura of quiet authority and profound depth. With eyes as silver as the moon's embrace, he gazes upon us with a serene wisdom that belies the countless eons he has witnessed. He is not just a guardian of knowledge but a key player in the cosmic war; his wisdom and guidance are crucial to our mission.

Each line etched upon his weathered face tells a story of epochs past, of civilizations risen and fallen, of knowledge sought and truths discovered. His countenance, bathed in the soft luminescence of celestial knowledge, seems to transcend the boundaries of mortal existence, hinting at the eternal truths that lie beyond.

As Thalios speaks, his voice resonates like the harmonies of the cosmos, carrying with it the echoes of a thousand lifetimes. It is a voice that has guided seekers and scholars alike through the annals of time, offering solace, enlightenment, and understanding to all who dare to tread the path of knowledge. Each word he utters is a beacon of truth, a key to unlocking the mysteries of the universe.

Clad in robes that seem to shimmer with the light of distant stars, Thalios stands as a beacon of enlightenment in the boundless expanse of the universe. His presence, a testament to the enduring power of wisdom, illuminates the path for those who seek to unravel the mysteries of existence.

This welcomes us into the sanctum of the library, where the air shimmers with ancient magick, his eyes vast as the cosmos, conveying a solemn message. "Greetings, Saturn, Miles," he begins, his voice echoing with the resonance of time. "I know why you've come through time and space. The threat posed by the Conclave of Shadows looms over both Earth and Eridanus, Saturn. Their nefarious plans endanger not only our existence but the very fabric of our lineage. Should they succeed, they will obliterate you and your unborn child, stripping away all your powers. Such a fate would grant them access to Eridanus once more, unleashing destruction upon everything we hold dear, including our ancestors and the light beings who call this realm home. Their insidious tactics have proven effective before; they decimated Atlantis and attempted the same with Eridanus, though they were thwarted in their efforts."

Thalios recounted the Conclave's deceptive rise to power, a tale woven with threads of betrayal and deceit. "In the case of Atlantis," he continued, his voice tinged with sorrow, "the Conclave's ascent was gradual, born from shadows and whispers. They masqueraded as allies, seeking assistance and guidance from the Atlanteans under false pretenses. Once their trust was gained, they seized the opportunity to plunder their artifacts, crystals, and powers, leaving destruction in their wake."

As I absorbed Thalios's account, a chill ran down my spine. The parallels between Atlantis's downfall and our current predicament were chilling. "They destroyed an entire civilization," I murmured, my voice barely above a whisper. "How can we hope to stand against such malevolence?"

Thalios's eyes softened with empathy, his unwavering determination shining through. "We must learn from history's mistakes," he declared, his voice echoing with resolve. "We cannot allow the Conclave to repeat their atrocities here. Together, we will forge a path to victory, one rooted in courage, unity, and unwavering determination."

At the realization, Saturn felt a chill run down her spine. "And Earth?" she asked, her heart heavy with foreboding.

Thalios's eyes gleamed with warning. "They seek to repeat their conquest on Earth; destroying all the star seed witches and leaving the humans on earth to dwell in the third dimension; unable to be guided towards any higher frequency—destroying any possibility of a new higher vibrational earth." he revealed. "But this time, they will not assault Eridanus directly, knowing they cannot breach its defenses. Instead, they target you, Saturn, aiming to seize your power and end the lineage, including your unborn child."

This, with the wisdom of ages etched into the lines of his face, stood as a beacon of guidance amidst the shadows of uncertainty that cloaked our path. His hands, trembling with the weight of foresight, hovered above a celestial map that shimmered like a tapestry woven from the very essence of the cosmos. The constellations, alien and mesmerizing, seemed to dance under his touch, revealing a journey that was as much a pilgrimage through the stars as it was a trial by fire.

"I am here to show you the path you seek and the way to the Arcanum Celestis," Thalios began, his voice steady and sure, a lighthouse in the stormy seas of our doubts. "The journey ahead is fraught with peril, yet it is the only way to unearth the tools and knowledge needed to dismantle the Conclave's dominion. Before you can wield the power of the Arcanum Celestis, you must embark on several quests, each leading you closer to the final artifact. These quests will test your strength, your resolve, and your very essence."

He spoke of the Arcanum Celestis with a reverence that filled the air with a palpable sense of destiny. Hidden within the depths of Eridanus, guarded by the spirits of the first Coven, this ancient artifact was the linchpin in our quest to unravel the Conclave's tyrannical grip. "This artifact," Thalios explained, his eyes gleaming with a mixture of hope and sorrow, "holds the key to understanding the Conclave's weaknesses and the secrets to their undoing.

But beware, for its power is coveted by many, friend and foe alike."

Miles, ever the embodiment of our collective apprehension, shifted uneasily. His concern was a mirror to our own, a reflection of the daunting path that lay ahead. "So, you're saying that this Arcanum Celestis is like a double-edged sword? It could help us, but it could also be a target for our enemies?"

Thalios's nod was solemn, a silent affirmation of the burdens we were to bear. "Indeed. The power it holds is immense, and in the wrong hands, it could tip the scales of the cosmic balance irreversibly."

The quest for the Arcanum Celestis, as Thalios outlined, was not a singular endeavor but a series of trials, each designed to prepare us for the ultimate confrontation. The first of these quests would take us to the edges of the known universe, where we were to retrieve the Celestial Compass from the ruins of a starship that had perished in the ancient cosmic wars. This compass, imbued with the ability to navigate the ethereal currents between worlds, was essential for charting our course through the celestial mazes that protected the Arcanum Celestis.

Following the compass, our journey would lead us to the Temple of the Starborn, a forgotten sanctuary where the Astral Codex was said to reside. The Codex, a tome of unfathomable knowledge, contained the incantations necessary to breach the Conclave's defenses and to commune with the spirits of the first Coven.

With the Celestial Compass to guide us and the Astral Codex to empower our magick, we would then seek the final piece before confronting the Arcanum Celestis itself: the Crystal of Eridani. This crystal, forged from the heart of a dying star, was the only material capable of containing the Arcanum's raw energy without succumbing to its corrupting influence.

Each quest, each artifact, was a step closer to our ultimate goal, a thread in the tapestry of our destiny that Thalios had unveiled. As we embarked on this journey, we carried with us not just the hope of our world but the immense weight of the cosmos, a responsibility that Thalios had entrusted upon us. The path to the Arcanum Celestis was more than a quest for power; it was a crusade for balance, a fight to restore the harmony of the universe that the Conclave sought to unravel.

In this awe-inspiring odyssey through the stars, we would not only discover the means to overcome our adversaries but also a profound understanding of the cosmic balance that governs all life. The Arcanum Celestis, a celestial artifact of unimaginable power and mystery, with its promise of enlightenment and its peril of temptation, stood as the ultimate testament to the dual nature of power: as a force for both creation and destruction, salvation, and damnation.

And so, with Thalios's words as our guide and the stars as our witnesses, we set forth on a journey that would lead us into the heart of darkness and the light of a new dawn.

The road ahead was uncertain, fraught with challenges that would test our very souls. But in the pursuit of the Arcanum Celestis, we found our purpose, our destiny intertwined with the fate of the cosmos itself, and a chance to thwart the Conclave's nefarious plans to disrupt the cosmic balance.

I shared a meaningful glance with Miles, my steadfast and trusted companion, a silent bond passing between us. We were not merely two adventurers on a quest; we were two souls united by a common purpose. This journey had indeed become more complex, but our resolve to restore balance to the cosmos remained unshakable.

"But fear not," Thalios continued, his tone reassuring. "With your courage and determination, I have faith that you will wield its power wisely and bring about the harmony that Eridanus so desperately seeks."

I took a deep breath, feeling a surge of determination coursing through my veins. "Thank you, Thalios. We won't let you down."

He offered us a gentle smile, his eyes twinkling with ancient wisdom. "Remember, Saturn and Miles, the fate of not just Eridanus, but all realms, here and on earth, rests in your hands. Trust in each other, and the light within you will guide the way."

With a final nod of appreciation, Miles and I rose to our feet, prepared to embark on the perilous journey that would shape the destiny of the cosmos. The burden of responsibility weighed heavily on our shoulders, but there was also a sense of anticipation in the air. We were aware that the path ahead was fraught with danger, from treacherous terrains to cunning adversaries. However, together, we would confront whatever challenges lay ahead and emerge triumphant, for the fate of the universe teetered on the edge.

As we prepared to embark on our quest, Thalios offered one final piece of wisdom, a mantra to carry in our hearts: "In the dance of light and shadow, it is balance that prevails. Seek harmony within yourselves, and the universe will align in your favor."

Amidst his profound guidance, Thalios reached into the depths of his cloak, retrieving an object that caught the dim light of the room and refracted it into a myriad of blues and violets. He opened his palm to reveal an iolite crystal, its surface a mesmerizing dance of deep indigo and sapphire, flecked with hints of golden sunlight. The crystal, no larger than a sparrow's egg, pulsed with an ethereal light as if holding the twilight sky within its core.

"This," Thalios said, his voice imbued with reverence, "is an iolite crystal, also known as the Viking's compass. It has the unique ability to guide its bearer through the thickest fogs and the darkest nights, pointing towards the artifacts you seek. Its hues mirror the heavens' own, a reminder that even in the darkest times, guidance is always at hand."

He placed the iolite gently in my palm, and its excellent

surface seemed to thrum with potential, a tangible connection to the ancient wisdom of the stars. "Let this be your guide," Thalios continued, "not just through the physical realms you will traverse, but through the inner journey you must undertake. The iolite will help you find the balance I speak of, its celestial colors a constant reminder of the harmony between light and shadow, and the path to aligning with the universe's vast energies."

With the iolite crystal, a tangible connection to the ancient wisdom of the stars, as our guide and Thalios's mantra etched in our hearts, we felt a renewed sense of purpose and clarity. The journey ahead promised challenges and trials, but with the wisdom of the Eridanus Coven, the guidance of Thalios, and the iolite crystal in hand, we were ready to face whatever lay ahead, our spirits buoyed by the promise of balance and alignment with the cosmos.

With dusk now entirely upon us, Miles and I stepped out of the ancient library, its walls lined with dusty tomes and the scent of old parchment lingering in the air. The crystal pulsated with a gentle light in my hand, casting a soft glow on our path. The quest had begun. Our mission was clear: to gather the ancient tools and unearth the knowledge that would lead to the Conclave's defeat. The path laid out by Thalios would take us through trials of courage, wisdom, and heart. But together, armed with the ancient wisdom of the Eridanus Coven and the guidance of Thalios, we were ready to face whatever lay ahead, our spirits united in the quest to restore balance to the cosmos. The air was thick with anticipation, the night sky a blanket of stars guiding our way.

"Miles," I whispered, my voice barely audible above the hum of the crystal. "Are you ready for this?"

He nodded, his expression resolute. "Absolutely, baby. We've come this far, haven't we? And with Thalios's guidance, I believe we can handle whatever challenges come our way."

As we set forth on our grand adventure, the weight of responsibility bears down on our shoulders, yet there's an undeniable thrill in the air. With each step we take, the crystal pulses with vibrant energy, guiding us deeper into the heart of Eridanus and drawing us closer to our fateful destiny.

"But first," I say, breaking the momentary silence, "we need to tell my Mother, Father and the ancestors what's going on, and bid them farewell."

In the sanctuary, surrounded by the comforting presence of my parents and the guiding spirits of our ancestors, Miles and I share the details of our encounter with Thalios and the daunting quest ahead.

As I recount the gravity of our conversation, there's a palpable sense of concern in the room, mingled with a glimmer of hope. My parents listen intently, their expressions reflecting a mixture of worry, determination, and a hint of pride in their child's bravery.

When I finish speaking, there's a moment of quiet

contemplation before my father speaks up. 'It's a perilous journey,' he acknowledges, his voice weighted with concern, 'a journey that will take you through treacherous lands, facing mythical creatures and ancient curses, but one that must be undertaken if you are to safeguard our lineage and our world.'

I nod, feeling the weight of our responsibility settle upon my shoulders. 'We understand the risks,' I reply, my voice echoing with unwavering determination, 'but with Thalios's guidance and our unyielding resolve, I believe we can face whatever challenges come our way.'

It's then that the ancestors' words echo in my mind, a reminder of the strength that lies within us. "Seek out the allies of light," they had urged, "for in unity there is strength."

As we step out of the sanctuary, a profound sense of purpose envelops me. The quest for the Arcanum Celestis is not a mere adventure; it's a solemn duty to protect our legacy and ensure the safety of our realm and earth.

Returning to our chambers, I catch Miles's gaze. His eyes reflect the same determination that burns within me.

"Are you ready for this?" he asks, his voice steady.

With a shared determination that binds us, I meet Miles's gaze and nod. "Absolutely," I reply, feeling the strength of our unity propel me forward.

Together, with the support of our family and ancestors, we'll face whatever challenges lie ahead. As we prepare to embark on our journey, I take a deep breath, steeling myself for the path that lies ahead. Whatever obstacles we may encounter, we'll face them head-on for the sake of our lineage and the prosperity of our world.

CHAPTER 3
THE CELESTIAL COMPASS

The night sky over Eridanus unfurls above me as I gaze up, marveling at the tapestry of cosmic splendor woven with constellations. The Eridanus constellation, a river of stars stretching across the heavens, feels like a celestial guide illuminated by luminous bodies that have shone for millennia. Each star, especially the radiant Achernar marking the river's end, whispers secrets from the past, urging Saturn and me onward in our quest for the Celestial Compass.

"Look at the night sky, Miles. See how Achernar shines, almost signaling our path. Each star along Eridanus's course seems to whisper secrets, urging us onward," Saturn muses aloud. Her voice is a mix of wonder and reverence for the celestial spectacle before us. The constellation, sprawling from the watery depths near Taurus and flowing past Orion, serves as a stellar guide, hinting at the mysteries waiting within the cosmos.

"Yeah, it's like they're guiding us to the Celestial Compass. Do you really think it's out here, hidden in some ancient starship?" I ask, my skepticism briefly overtaken by awe. The vast expanse of Eridanus, with its assembly of stars, bridges, myth, and reality, suggests untold secrets and ancient lore that might be discovered in the relics of a civilization that once navigated this cosmic river.

"I believe so. Thalios's wisdom and the crystal's light haven't led us astray yet. We're on the right path," Saturn affirms, her confidence bolstered by our guidance.

At the launch pad on the edge of the Eridanus sector, Saturn and I stand before our spacecraft, a marvel of engineering designed for velocity and the intricate dance among the stars. The ship sits quietly, its hull catching the starlight and reflecting it, creating an effect akin to gazing into the night sky itself. This mimicry of the cosmos on its surface makes the ship seem less like a vehicle and more like an extension of the universe waiting to be explored. The excitement of piloting it buzzes through me, a mix of exhilaration and apprehension. Neither of us has navigated a ship through the cosmic sea before, and the thought of guiding this embodiment of speed and precision through the celestial void is both an honor and a daunting challenge.

As I approached the pilot's seat, anticipation washed over me. The cockpit, with its array of unfamiliar controls and displays, presented a challenge. Yet, the seat itself, designed to link directly with the pilot's neural pathways, hints at possibilities we hadn't considered.

"Look at the sky, Miles. Achernar's glow seems almost like a sign," Saturn says, her voice blending awe and resolve. Indeed, the constellations weave a path for us, a celestial map leading to our destiny.

"Can we really navigate this craft, guided by the stars and these cosmic whispers?" I ponder aloud. The challenge seems immense, but as we tentatively reach out with our thoughts toward the ship's controls, something extraordinary happens.

The craft responds with a soft hum, not to physical touch, but to our intentions. The revelation is both empowering and exhilarating; the ship is telepathically linked to us, moving in harmony with our desires.

"Miles, it's responding to our thoughts!" Saturn exclaims, her voice mirroring my excitement.

"This is incredible," I can't help but agree, grinning. "We don't need traditional piloting skills; we simply have to think about our destination, and the craft will take us there." This discovery transforms our journey from a daunting task into an exhilarating adventure.

With focused intention, the craft lifts off seamlessly, propelling us into the cosmos. The outpost recedes behind us as we venture into the infinite, our path illuminated by the stars of Eridanus and guided by the power of our minds.

As we approach the ancient vessel, a relic pinpointed by the faithful luminescence of the iolite crystal, the profound sense of history etched into its hull strikes us. "The marks of time and conflict... They serve as a solemn reminder of the events this ship has witnessed," I reflect, awed by its silent testament.

"Yet, it's now the custodian of something truly priceless. Are you ready to uncover what secrets it's been keeping?" Saturn counters with an excited gleam in her eye.

Guided by the iolite crystal, we make our way inside the ship. The airlock's hiss ushers us into a realm frozen in time, where the echoes of a bygone era linger.

Inside, the vessel unfolds like a cryptic maze. Our lights reveal intricate craftsmanship, a sight that leaves us in silent reverence.

"Can you believe this, Saturn? It's like we've stepped across a threshold into history," I whisper, awed by our surroundings.

"No, I've never seen anything like it. Every corner of this ship tells a story, waiting for us to listen," she replies, equally mesmerized.

We venture deeper, finding the control room and, at its heart, our prize: the Celestial Compass, its energy resonating with a promise of journeys yet to come.

"There's the Celestial Compass, just as incredible as we hoped," I point out, barely containing my anticipation.

"It's beautiful. The symbols, the glow... it feels like it's alive, connecting me to the cosmos in ways I can't explain,"

Saturn whispers, lifting the Celestial Compass. Its glow seems to breathe, connecting us to the cosmos in profound ways.

"The vision it's showing us... the Temple of the Starborn. This is the path we need to follow," I state, understanding dawning on me as the artifact reveals our next destination.

"Yes, and we must hurry. The Compass is awake, eager to lead us. The asteroid field now seems like a minor obstacle," Saturn agrees, urgency lacing her words as we prepare to depart.

"To the Temple of the Starborn then. This is just the beginning, Saturn. The Celestial Compass is the key to more than we imagined," I say with determination, setting our sights on the Temple.

"Every artifact brings us closer to our goal. The Conclave doesn't stand a chance," Saturn declares, bolstered by our successes.

"We've got this. Together, there's nothing we can't overcome. The balance of the cosmos is in our hands," I affirm, meeting her gaze with unwavering resolve.

"With the light within us and the guidance of the stars, we will restore balance. To Eridanus, Earth, and beyond," she vows, the magnitude of our mission resonating within us.

"Let's continue our quest—for courage, wisdom, and the light that guides us through the darkness," I conclude. Together, we embark on the next chapter of our journey, hearts full and spirits lifted by the knowledge that each step draws us nearer to our ultimate goal. Our quest for the Arcanum Celestis continues, a beacon of hope in the darkness, a testament to the enduring power of courage, wisdom, and the unyielding light of the stars.

CHAPTER 4
THE ASTRAL CODEX

With the Celestial Compass firmly in our hands, Miles and I set our course toward the Temple of the Starborn, concealed within the awe-inspiring expanse of a nebula known as the Veil of Dreams. The scene that unfolds before us is a breathtaking spectacle, a vast canvas of cosmic beauty that seems to throb with life, evoking a sense of wonder and awe in our hearts.

"Can you believe we're actually on the path to the Temple of the Starborn?" I find myself whispering, my voice trembling with sheer wonder. The nebula before us, the Veil of Dreams, blooms like a celestial flower, its vibrant hues and swirling mists painting a scene that feels both surreal and inviting.

"It's more incredible than I imagined," Miles replies, his voice filled with awe. As I gaze into the heart of the nebula,

I can't help but agree. Each star that dots this cosmic garden emits a soft glow, casting light on the nebula's swirling clouds, which shift from deep purples to vibrant pinks and serene blues. It's as if every color imaginable has found a place here, blending in a mesmerizing dance of light and shadow.

The vastness of the nebula engulfs us, a testament to the universe's boundless beauty and enigma. "Every star, every hue in that nebula feels like it's embracing us," I continue, feeling a profound connection to this place. The Veil of Dreams seems alive, its ever-shifting patterns and radiant depths drawing us closer to our destination, fostering a sense of belonging and involvement in our cosmic journey.

As we approach, the very fabric of the nebula wraps around us, guiding our path. It's a moment of pure anticipation, a reminder of the infinite possibilities that lie within the universe. The Temple of the Starborn, concealed somewhere within this celestial masterpiece, beckons us, promising to unveil secrets of the cosmos that we have yet to fathom, stirring a sense of curiosity and excitement within us.

Guided by the ethereal glow of the Compass, our ship cuts through the fabric of space, a lone beacon amidst the boundless darkness.

"The Celestial Compass has guided us well," I acknowledge, my voice filled with gratitude. "Without it, finding this place would have been an insurmountable challenge."

As the Temple of the Starborn materializes from the

nebula's core, it's as if the very fabric of the universe has been woven into its structure. The temple stands majestic, a silent guardian amidst the cosmic dance, with spires that reach towards the heavens, each one kissed by the luminescence of stardust. Its arches curve gracefully, framing the void beyond in a display of celestial craftsmanship. Their surfaces catch the nebula's light and scatter it in a thousand directions, creating a spectacle of shimmering brilliance.

"Look at the architecture of the temple. It's like something out of a dream," Miles comments, his voice filled with awe. His words barely capture the ethereal beauty that unfolds before us. The temple's design transcends the boundaries of imagination, its intricate details and towering edifices suggesting an otherworldly origin. It stands not just as a structure but as a testament to the sublime artistry of the Starborn, its creators.

Stepping onto the temple's outer platform, we feel the sensation of stepping into another realm. The air here thrums with a palpable energy, a resonance of ancient magick that seems to pulsate through the very ground beneath our feet. The entrance, a grand archway flanked by statues of the Starborn, beckons us forward. These statues, majestic and imposing, are not mere stone but seem to be carved from the essence of light itself. They stand as silent sentinels, their faces serene, eyes aglow with an inner radiance that speaks of wisdom and power beyond comprehension. It's as though these beings of pure energy and light have been forever immortalized, watching over the threshold between worlds, guardians of the mysteries that lie within.

Each step we take closer to the entrance amplifies the sense of awe and reverence. The Temple of the Starborn, rising majestically from the heart of the nebula, is not merely a destination but a portal to the depths of the cosmos, inviting us to uncover the secrets it has safeguarded through the ages.

"These statues... the Starborn. They feel alive, watching over this sanctuary," I note, sensing the deep, inner luminescence of their crystal eyes.

"It's eerie but fascinating," Miles agrees. "Their eyes seem to know we're here for a purpose."

The Compass leads us unerringly through the temple's maze of corridors and chambers, each adorned with celestial motifs and inscriptions.

Navigating the labyrinthine passageways of the temple, I felt an unspoken urgency quicken my steps. The Compass, a relic of incalculable antiquity and precision, guided us unerringly. Its needle, luminous and unwavering, pointed the way forward through a network of corridors and chambers, each more opulently decorated than the last. The walls were adorned with celestial motifs—spiraling galaxies, constellations in mid-dance, and planets in various phases of orbit. Inscriptions in a script that shimmered like stardust covered the surfaces; their meanings were known only to those initiated into the deepest mysteries of the cosmos.

"The Codex must be close," Miles murmured, breaking the reverent silence that had fallen between us. His voice echoed slightly in the expansive heart of the temple, a grand chamber where the air itself seemed saturated with ancient power. At the center, where the Astral Codex was believed to reside, stood a pedestal crafted from pure obsidian, its surface smooth and reflective as a still lake under moonlight.

Approaching the pedestal, I felt the air thrum with energy, a silent hum that resonated in the marrow of my bones. The Compass quivered in my hand, its needle spinning briefly before settling pointedly towards the Codex. I reached out, my hands trembling with a cocktail of anticipation and reverence. The cover of the Codex was a masterpiece of craftsmanship, adorned with cosmic symbols and inlaid with gems that caught the dim light, casting prisms across the dark stone of the chamber.

Gently, I opened the Codex. A brilliant light immediately flooded the chamber, pure and white, as if a star had been born within the confines of these ancient walls. The light was warm, its touch ethereal, and as it enveloped us, the room expanded beyond its physical boundaries into a realm that transcended time and space.

Within the pages of the Astral Codex lay the collective wisdom of the Starborn, beings whose knowledge spanned the aeons. As I turned each page, visions flashed before my eyes—ancient rituals conducted under the watchful eyes of celestial bodies, forgotten magicks that whispered of boundless power, and deep, enduring mysteries that had puzzled the greatest minds of many a civilization. These were not merely words and images; they were experiences, memories imprinted on the very essence of the universe itself.

With each page, I felt as though I was drifting further from my reality, caught in the gravitational pull of knowledge so profound it threatened to overwhelm my understanding. Miles stood beside me, equally captivated, his eyes wide with wonder and a thirst for understanding that mirrored my own.

I can see the change in you, Saturn," Miles watches, awestruck. "It's like the Codex is speaking directly to your soul."

Among the secrets unveiled, a ritual to amplify our powers and breach the Conclave's defenses shines brightest.

"That sounds powerful. And dangerous," Miles comments, understanding the significance of what we've discovered.

"But necessary," I assert. "We need every advantage we can get."

As we navigate back through the temple's corridors, I feel a profound connection to the Starborn, their legacy now interwoven with our quest.

"The Starborn's legacy, it's with us now," I shared with Miles. "Their wisdom, their strength... It's part of our quest."

Glancing back at the Veil of Dreams, the journey feels both monumental and transformative.

"With the Compass and the Codex, we're one step closer to facing the Conclave," I reflect, feeling the weight of our mission.

"And we'll go further," Miles adds confidently. "The Crystal of Eridani is next. Are you ready for what comes after?"

"As ready as we'll ever be," I affirm. "The Codex has prepared us, and together, we're unstoppable."

With each artifact recovered and each secret unearthed, our journey through the cosmos continues, a testament to the enduring power of hope, the unbreakable bond of unity, and the indomitable spirit of those committed to restoring balance to the universe.

CHAPTER 5
THE CRYSTAL OF ERIDANI

With the wisdom of the Astral Codex woven into the fabric of my destiny, Miles and I set our sights on the final leg of our intro to the Arcanum Celestis: the quest for the Crystal of Eridani.

"Feels like we're on the cusp of something monumental, doesn't it?" I look over at Miles as our ship pierces through the cosmos, guided by the Celestial Compass.

"It does. Hard to believe we're about to retrieve a shard of a star," Miles replies, his gaze fixed on the vastness outside, where light fights against the dark veil of space.

Our voyage takes us beyond the familiar constellations, deep into the remnants of the Eridani star system, now overshadowed by the omnipresent pull of a black hole. The sensation of the ship trembling under the black hole's immense gravitational force is a stark reminder of the cosmic forces at play. "The gravity of that black hole... it's intense," I note aloud, feeling the subtle vibrations through the deck under our feet.

Miles, with his hands resting lightly on the controls, nods in agreement. Yet, it's his focus and intent that guide our ship, not the physical manipulation of instruments. "But we've got this. The connection I have with the ship through my thoughts, plus your insights from the Codex? We're more than just a team," he assures me, his confidence steadying. Our journey, propelled by Miles' thoughts and the ship's response to his silent commands, weaves through the cosmic dangers with a grace that belies our initial apprehension.

As we descend onto what was once the vibrant heart of the Eridani system, the landscape greets us mesmerizingly. The surface shimmers with the residual energy of a star-long fade, casting an ethereal light over the ruins. "This place is charged with history," I whisper, each word heavy with the weight of a bygone era's legacy.

"And power," Miles adds, his gaze fixed on the horizon where the Crystal of Eridani lies.

In the heart of what was once the vibrant Eridani system, amidst the ruins shadowed by the colossal force of the black hole, lies the Crystal of Eridani. As we approach, the artifact reveals itself not merely as an object of beauty but as a relic of immense power, a shard of a star that once illuminated this part of the cosmos. The Crystal pulses with a light that is both serene and intense, its glow a testament to the star's enduring legacy.

The Crystal of Eridani, nestled within the remnants of its celestial progenitor, radiates with the energy of a bygone era. Its surface, multifaceted and shimmering, captures the very essence of the cosmos. Light dances across its edges, casting colorful patterns on the ground around us, a silent symphony of color and motion that mesmerizes and enchants.

"It recognizes the journey we've undertaken," I say, struck by the profound connection that seems to form instantaneously between me and the artifact. The Crystal, though a mere shard, embodies the heart of a star, its energies resonant with the forces that drive the universe itself.

Holding the Crystal of Eridani in my hands, I feel its warmth, a gentle yet powerful reminder of its origin. The shard vibrates with the remnants of the stellar fire, a core once ablaze with nuclear fusion, now tranquil yet potent in its silent vigil. The light it emits is not merely illumination but a beacon of balance and harmony, echoing the star's life-giving radiance.

"The visions it's granting you," Miles remarks, his voice filled with awe and curiosity. Indeed, the Crystal offers more than light; it unveils the fabric of the universe, revealing the intricate dance of galaxies, the birth of stars, and the delicate threads that connect all forms of existence.

"They are," I confirm. The Crystal, now in our hands,

unveils the fabric of the universe in ways both overwhelming and enlightening. Its glow offers glimpses into the cosmic dance of creation and destruction, a balance we are now a part of.

With the Crystal securely within our grasp, a sense of purpose solidifies between us. "We're not just adventurers," Miles reflects, the journey's weight settling in. "We're catalysts for change."

Our voyage, initially a foray into the unknown guided by the developing bond between Miles' intent and our ship, has brought us to the heart of Eridani. Here, amidst the echoes of a star's life and death, the Crystal of Eridani in our possession stands as a testament to our role in the universe's grand tapestry. Our mission, far from complete, is a journey not just through space but through the potential that lies within us and the ship that responds to Miles' guiding thoughts, leading us toward our destiny.

As we prepare to return, the significance of our mission is palpable. "The artifacts... they're more than just tools. They're a testament to our journey," I state, feeling a surge of resolve.

Our trip back to Eridanus is quiet and reflective. "The Arcanum Celestis is within reach now. Do you think we're ready?" Miles asks, his voice tinged with anticipation.

"We have to be firm in our belief," I responded. The Codex, the Compass, the Crystal... they've all led us to this moment."

Under the vast expanse of the Eridanus sky, now safely back on solid ground with our spacecraft nestled quietly behind us, Miles and I share a moment of calm before the storm. The engines have cooled, and the ship, our companion through countless light-years and cosmic wonders, sits silently, a testament to the journey we've undertaken. "This battle against the Conclave," I muse, gazing up at the stars, "it's for the essence of the universe itself." The quiet of Eridanus envelops us, a brief respite in the shadow of the looming conflict.

Miles catches a thoughtful look I cast downward, the gesture not lost on him. He breaks the silence with a gentle inquiry. "We've been so caught up in our quest, but how have you been feeling, my love? With the baby on the way, I mean," he asks, concern and curiosity mixing in his voice. It's a moment that grounds us, a reminder of the life we're nurturing even as we navigate the uncertainties of our mission.

I let out a soft sigh, the tranquility of our surroundings on Eridanus offering a stark contrast to the turmoil of our journey. "It's been a whirlwind, hasn't it?" I reply, my hand instinctively resting on my belly, and the subtle movements beneath my palm are a constant reassurance. "But despite everything, I feel... hopeful. This baby, our child, is a beacon of hope for the future we're fighting to secure."

Miles nods, his eyes reflecting the starlight, a blend of resolve and warmth in his gaze. "A new beginning," he agrees, the soft hum of the night around us lending weight to his words. I've been so focused on piloting us through the stars, but knowing we're bringing a new life into this universe adds a layer of purpose to our journey I hadn't fully realized."

Our conversation, amidst the backdrop of Eridanus' serene beauty and the tranquility of our landed ship, shifts our focus from the cosmic scale of our mission to the personal significance of our growing family. "Our child will grow up surrounded by stories of our journey, tales of wonders beyond imagination," I say, envisioning the future. "And no matter the outcome of our battle against the Conclave, we'll ensure they inherit a legacy of courage, wisdom, and the unyielding light of the stars."

Miles takes my hand, his touch conveying strength and reassurance. "Together, we'll face whatever comes. For the essence of the universe, for the future of our child," he vows, his commitment ringing clear under the starlit sky of Eridanus.

As we stand together, the gentle breeze carrying the whispers of distant worlds, the challenges ahead seem less daunting. With our ship safely harbored and the endless sky above as our witness, we're reminded that our fight is not just for the balance of the cosmos but for the future of our family. In this quiet corner of Eridanus, under the watchful gaze of the stars, our resolve is renewed, fortified by the promise of new life and the enduring hope that guides us.

As dawn ushers in the day of our final endeavor, Miles and I share a profound sense of unity. "The Arcanum Celestis is within our reach. Together, we'll bring an end to the tyranny," I state with conviction, the Crystal Compass and Iolite Crystal lighting the way through the depths of Eridanus, where ancient secrets and powers lay hidden.

"The challenges we face will be significant," Miles concedes, his voice steady and resolved. "Yet, we are equipped—ready to confront what lies ahead for the sake of the cosmos and the delicate balance we vow to protect."

As we venture deeper into the forest of Eridanus, guided by the Crystal Compass and Iolite Crystal, the significance of our mission becomes ever more palpable. "This is the moment, Miles. Here, where our quest may find its end, our true journey begins. As defenders of light and the harbingers of balance," I proclaim, my resolve firm. With Miles at my side, we advance, poised to uncover the Arcanum Celestis, the key to dismantling the Conclave's oppressive rule.

The anticipation of uncovering the Arcanum Celestis, hidden and protected by the ancient wisdom of the first Coven, imbues us with a sense of purpose and destiny. This sacred artifact, harboring the knowledge to expose the Conclave's vulnerabilities and the means to their downfall, beckons us closer.

"Our story, intertwined with the fate of the universe, is far from over," I reflect. With the promise of new beginnings and the hope of restoring equilibrium, Miles and I press on, champions of a cause greater than ourselves, guided by the legacy of those who came before us. Our quest for the Arcanum Celestis may be reaching its climax, but the narrative we share, rich with courage, wisdom, and the pursuit of balance, continues to unfold under the watchful gaze of the cosmos.

CHAPTER 6

THE ARCANUM CELESTIS

Miles and I delved deeper into the dense, whispering forest of Eridanus, each step taken on the vibrant tapestry of foliage that carpeted the ground beneath the celestial glow of the sky. The Crystal Compass and Iolite Crystal, our steadfast guides, led us with a luminescence that sliced through the shadowy underbrush, hinting at the path we were meant to follow through this ancient woodland.

"The forest itself seems to be guiding us now," I remarked to Miles, my voice a soft echo amidst the chorus of nocturnal life and the gentle rustling of leaves. There was an undeniable sense of anticipation in the air, a feeling that we were not merely walking on solid ground but traversing the annals of time and mystery. My heart raced with a mix of excitement and trepidation, mirroring the unknown path ahead.

"It certainly does," Miles concurred, his eyes reflecting the myriad shades of green and twilight that enveloped us. "And it's taking us somewhere extraordinary. Can you feel that?"

Following the beacon light of our crystals, we eventually came upon a concealed descent—a staircase hewn from the very essence of the earth, spiraling down into the depths. The temperature dropped as we descended, our crystal lights casting eerie shadows against the ancient stone. With each step, our hearts quickened, the anticipation of what lay ahead almost palpable.

The stairway opened into a colossal underground chamber, an otherworldly sanctuary illuminated by a constellation of bioluminescent fungi. The fungi, their soft glow casting a surreal light, clung to the walls and ceiling, creating a breathtaking sight. Towering stalactites and stalagmites, some as thick as ancient trees, formed a stone forest around us, their silhouettes bathed in an ethereal glow.

And there, in the heart of this underground cathedral, sat the Arcanum Celestis. Unlike any artifact we had encountered on our journey, it defied all expectations—a singular object of pure gold, floating serenely above a pedestal that seemed to have grown from the very bedrock to cradle it. The Arcanum Celestis pulsed with a soft, golden light, casting warm, illuminating rays that touched every corner of the chamber. Its surface was etched with intricate symbols and glyphs that danced under its glow, a visual symphony of knowledge and power.

"We've found it, Miles. The Arcanum Celestis," I whispered, my voice filled with a mixture of reverence and disbelief. Together, we approached, drawn by the irresistible pull of the artifact's ancient energy.

As my fingers grazed the golden surface, the chamber thrummed with resonant power. The Arcanum Celestis awakened fully at our touch, its brilliance intensifying. The symbols etched upon it began to move, to tell their stories —revealing the Conclave's vulnerabilities, the secrets of their power, and the keys to their undoing.

"It's incredible," Miles whispered, captivated by the artifact's display. "It's showing us everything we need to know."

Holding the Arcanum Celestis, I realized its uniqueness lay not only in its composition but in its purpose. "This is more than an artifact; it's the embodiment of hope, the beacon that will guide us to victory," I declared, feeling its weight as a tangible promise of the future we were striving to create.

As we retraced our steps back to the surface, the Arcanum Celestis in hand, a renewed sense of determination surged within us. "With this, we can end the Conclave's reign," I declared, my voice resonating with unwavering conviction. The artifact, with its golden glow and revealing light, had armed us with knowledge and power beyond our wildest dreams, fueling our resolve to change the course of our world.

Emerging from the underground, the Eridanian forest greets us once more, the stars above brighter than ever. With the Arcanum Celestis as our guide, Miles and I are ready to face the challenges ahead. Our mission, far from over, is now imbued with a deeper purpose. Armed with the secrets unveiled by the golden artifact, we step forward into the night, ready to change the course of the cosmos. Our journey for balance and freedom continues—powered by the glow of the Arcanum Celestis, a testament to the enduring strength of hope, courage, and the light that guides us through the darkest times. The challenges we face are not just physical but also philosophical as we grapple with the nature of balance and interconnectedness in the vastness of the cosmos.

"Can you believe this is it, Saturn? The final chapter," Miles whispers, his voice thick with emotion as we stand ready, the Celestial Compass, the Astral Codex, the Crystal of Eridani, and the Arcanum Celestis in hand. The weight of our journey, the joy of our discoveries, and the anticipation of what lies ahead are all palpable in his voice.

"The artifacts... they've been more than guides; they've been companions on this journey," I reply, feeling the weight of our destiny pulsing through them.

Back at the Sanctuary, where magick seamlessly weaves into the fabric of reality, Miles and I are warmly greeted by my parents, Willow and Sebastian, along with an assembly of ancestors and luminous beings. Their radiant and welcoming presence, a testament to the strength of our family bond, fills the air with a sense of completion and continuity as we stand on the verge of returning home through the crystal archway portal.

Willow, her eyes brimming with the wisdom of eons, embraces us both. "Your journey has shown you all the interconnectedness of the universe, how every action, every decision weaves into the cosmic tapestry," she shares, her voice echoing the depths of the cosmos itself.

Sebastian, with a twinkle in his eye, adds, "And let's not forget the practical side of things. You've probably learned a few tricks about keeping those cosmic connections in balance, eh?" His laughter is a grounding force, reminding us of the lighter moments amidst our profound quest.

Miles, glancing at me with a knowing smile, reflects on our journey. "It's incredible, isn't it? How this quest has taught us about the interconnectedness of everything. The universe is a vast web, and we're just one strand in it." His words, filled with wonder and awe, echo the sentiments of our shared journey.

I nod, feeling the truth of his words resonate deep within. "Yes, and it's shown us that by restoring balance in one part, we help bring harmony to the whole. Every star, every planet, every life form is connected in ways we're just beginning to understand."

As we walk with our family and the assembled beings toward the portal, the conversations flow around us, a melding of past wisdom and present experience. My parents and ancestors share tales of their journeys, each story a thread in the intricate fabric of existence, highlighting the endless connections that bind us all. At this moment, we are not just a group of individuals but a united force bound by our shared understanding of the cosmic web and our commitment to protect its balance.

Standing before the shimmering portal, the artifacts in our possession begin to resonate, a physical manifestation of the universal harmony we've been discussing. "Look, the Compass, the Codex, the Crystal, the Arcanum... they're all reacting," I can't help but marvel. The sight of our artifacts, each a key to unraveling the mysteries of the cosmos, harmonizing together, underscores the lesson of our quest —that every element of the universe is intricately connected, each piece vital to the whole. Their ethereal glow and the hum of their power fill the air, sparking a sense of wonder and awe in our hearts.

Miles, his eyes alight with the wonder of our discoveries, turns to me, his hand squeezing mine. "Ready to float through time and space again, baby?" he asks, his voice laced with the excitement of embarking on another journey through the unknown yet familiar pathways of the cosmos.

"Always, as long as it's with you," I reply, my heart swelling with love and a newfound understanding of our place in the universe. As we step through the portal, enveloped in the light of our harmonizing artifacts, we're not just traversing physical distances; we're moving through the web of connections that unites all existence.

Our passage through the portal is a journey through the heart of existence itself, a reminder of the interconnectedness that Willow spoke of, and a visual testament to the universal balance we're sworn to protect. As we emerge on the other side, back to Nightshade Mansion, we carry with us not only the artifacts but a more profound knowledge of the cosmic web that binds everything together.

The quest for the Arcanum Celestis might have reached its physical end, but the lessons we've learned about the interconnectedness of the universe and our role within it will continue to guide us. As we face the challenges ahead, Miles and I do so with the understanding that in restoring balance to one part, we contribute to the harmony of the whole. Our journey as guardians of light and protectors of balance is just beginning, driven by the conviction that everything in the universe is connected, and every action we take ripples through the cosmos, shaping the destiny of all. This journey, this adventure, has not only tested our physical and mental strength but also our understanding of ourselves and our place in the universe, and it has made us stronger, wiser, and more connected to the world around us.

Miles and I delved deeper into the dense, whispering forest of Eridanus, each step taken on the vibrant tapestry of foliage that carpeted the ground beneath the celestial glow of the sky. The Crystal Compass and Iolite Crystal, our steadfast guides, led us with a luminescence that sliced through the shadowy underbrush, hinting at the path we were meant to follow through this ancient woodland.

"The forest itself seems to be guiding us now," I remarked to Miles, my voice a soft echo amidst the chorus of nocturnal life and the gentle rustling of leaves. There was an undeniable sense of anticipation in the air, a feeling that we were not merely walking on solid ground but traversing the annals of time and mystery. My heart raced with a mix of excitement and trepidation, mirroring the unknown path ahead.

"It certainly does," Miles concurred, his eyes reflecting the myriad shades of green and twilight that enveloped us. "And it's taking us somewhere extraordinary. Can you feel that?"

Following the beacon light of our crystals, we eventually came upon a concealed descent—a staircase hewn from the very essence of the earth, spiraling down into the depths. The temperature dropped as we descended, our crystal lights casting eerie shadows against the ancient stone. With each step, our hearts quickened, the anticipation of what lay ahead almost palpable.

The stairway opened into a colossal underground chamber, an otherworldly sanctuary illuminated by a constellation of bioluminescent fungi. The fungi, their soft glow casting a surreal light, clung to the walls and ceiling, creating a breathtaking sight. Towering stalactites and stalagmites, some as thick as ancient trees, formed a stone forest around us, their silhouettes bathed in an ethereal glow.

And there, in the heart of this underground cathedral, sat the Arcanum Celestis. Unlike any artifact we had encountered on our journey, it defied all expectations—a singular object of pure gold, floating serenely above a pedestal that seemed to have grown from the very bedrock to cradle it. The Arcanum Celestis pulsed with a soft, golden light, casting warm, illuminating rays that touched every corner of the chamber. Its surface was etched with intricate symbols and glyphs that danced under its glow, a visual symphony of knowledge and power.

"We've found it, Miles. The Arcanum Celestis," I whispered, my voice filled with a mixture of reverence and disbelief. Together, we approached, drawn by the irresistible pull of the artifact's ancient energy.

As my fingers grazed the golden surface, the chamber thrummed with resonant power. The Arcanum Celestis awakened fully at our touch, its brilliance intensifying. The symbols etched upon it began to move, to tell their stories —revealing the Conclave's vulnerabilities, the secrets of their power, and the keys to their undoing.

"It's incredible," Miles whispered, captivated by the artifact's display. "It's showing us everything we need to know."

Holding the Arcanum Celestis, I realized its uniqueness lay not only in its composition but in its purpose. "This is more than an artifact; it's the embodiment of hope, the beacon that will guide us to victory," I declared, feeling its weight as a tangible promise of the future we were striving to create.

As we retraced our steps back to the surface, the Arcanum Celestis in hand, a renewed sense of determination surged within us. "With this, we can end the Conclave's reign," I declared, my voice resonating with unwavering conviction. The artifact, with its golden glow and revealing light, had armed us with knowledge and power beyond our wildest dreams, fueling our resolve to change the course of our world.

Emerging from the underground, the Eridanian forest greets us once more, the stars above brighter than ever. With the Arcanum Celestis as our guide, Miles and I are ready to face the challenges ahead. Our mission, far from over, is now imbued with a deeper purpose. Armed with the secrets unveiled by the golden artifact, we step forward into the night, ready to change the course of the cosmos. Our journey for balance and freedom continues—powered by the glow of the Arcanum Celestis, a testament to the enduring strength of hope, courage, and the light that guides us through the darkest times. The challenges we face are not just physical but also philosophical as we grapple with the nature of balance and interconnectedness in the vastness of the cosmos.

"Can you believe this is it, Saturn? The final chapter," Miles whispers, his voice thick with emotion as we stand ready, the Celestial Compass, the Astral Codex, the Crystal of Eridani, and the Arcanum Celestis in hand. The weight of our journey, the joy of our discoveries, and the anticipation of what lies ahead are all palpable in his voice.

"The artifacts... they've been more than guides; they've been companions on this journey," I reply, feeling the weight of our destiny pulsing through them.

Back at the Sanctuary, where magick seamlessly weaves into the fabric of reality, Miles and I are warmly greeted by my parents, Willow and Sebastian, along with an assembly of ancestors and luminous beings. Their radiant and welcoming presence, a testament to the strength of our family bond, fills the air with a sense of completion and continuity as we stand on the verge of returning home through the crystal archway portal.

Willow, her eyes brimming with the wisdom of eons, embraces us both. "Your journey has shown you all the interconnectedness of the universe, how every action, every decision weaves into the cosmic tapestry," she shares, her voice echoing the depths of the cosmos itself.

Sebastian, with a twinkle in his eye, adds, "And let's not forget the practical side of things. You've probably learned a few tricks about keeping those cosmic connections in balance, eh?" His laughter is a grounding force, reminding us of the lighter moments amidst our profound quest.

Miles, glancing at me with a knowing smile, reflects on our journey. "It's incredible, isn't it? How this quest has taught us about the interconnectedness of everything. The universe is a vast web, and we're just one strand in it." His words, filled with wonder and awe, echo the sentiments of our shared journey.

I nod, feeling the truth of his words resonate deep within. "Yes, and it's shown us that by restoring balance in one part, we help bring harmony to the whole. Every star, every planet, every life form is connected in ways we're just beginning to understand."

As we walk with our family and the assembled beings toward the portal, the conversations flow around us, a melding of past wisdom and present experience. My parents and ancestors share tales of their journeys, each story a thread in the intricate fabric of existence, highlighting the endless connections that bind us all. At this moment, we are not just a group of individuals but a united force bound by our shared understanding of the cosmic web and our commitment to protect its balance.

Standing before the shimmering portal, the artifacts in our possession begin to resonate, a physical manifestation of the universal harmony we've been discussing. "Look, the Compass, the Codex, the Crystal, the Arcanum... they're all reacting," I can't help but marvel. The sight of our artifacts, each a key to unraveling the mysteries of the cosmos, harmonizing together, underscores the lesson of our quest —that every element of the universe is intricately connected, each piece vital to the whole. Their ethereal glow and the hum of their power fill the air, sparking a sense of wonder and awe in our hearts.

Miles, his eyes alight with the wonder of our discoveries, turns to me, his hand squeezing mine. "Ready to float through time and space again, baby?" he asks, his voice laced with the excitement of embarking on another journey through the unknown yet familiar pathways of the cosmos.

"Always, as long as it's with you," I reply, my heart swelling with love and a newfound understanding of our place in the universe. As we step through the portal, enveloped in the light of our harmonizing artifacts, we're not just traversing physical distances; we're moving through the web of connections that unites all existence.

Our passage through the portal is a journey through the heart of existence itself, a reminder of the interconnectedness that Willow spoke of, and a visual testament to the universal balance we're sworn to protect. As we emerge on the other side, back to Nightshade Mansion, we carry with us not only the artifacts but a more profound knowledge of the cosmic web that binds everything together.

The quest for the Arcanum Celestis might have reached its physical end, but the lessons we've learned about the interconnectedness of the universe and our role within it will continue to guide us. As we face the challenges ahead, Miles and I do so with the understanding that in restoring balance to one part, we contribute to the harmony of the whole. Our journey as guardians of light and protectors of balance is just beginning, driven by the conviction that everything in the universe is connected, and every action we take ripples through the cosmos, shaping the destiny of all. This journey, this adventure, has not only tested our physical and mental strength but also our understanding of ourselves and our place in the universe, and it has made us stronger, wiser, and more connected to the world around us.

CHAPTER 7

RETURN TO EARTH

As Miles and I step through the portal, Earth's familiar embrace surrounds us instantly. The portal's closure, a soft whoosh in the background, marks our departure from the vast cosmos back to the tangible reality of our home. The sudden shift from the boundless universe to the tranquil woods around Nightshade Mansion is disorienting. Here, the scent of pine and moist Earth grounds us, a stark contrast to the cosmic energies we've been immersed in.

With no time to spare, we rush toward the mansion, driven by an urgency that has become second nature to us. The silhouette of Nightshade Mansion, with its intricate gothic spires, stands as a testament to the countless secrets and stories it harbors.

The moment we burst through the front doors, Lysandra's cry of shock and relief echoes through the grand entrance. She stands at the foot of the staircase, her expression oscillating between disbelief and joy.

"You're back!" she exclaims, voice laced with emotion. "I've been so freakin' worried about you guys! You vanished for a whole month!"

Miles and I look confused. "A month?" I repeat, struggling to align our perception of time with Earth's reality. "But for us, it's only been a week."

Miles steps forward, his voice tinged with concern. "I guess time flows differently between the realms. We didn't realize... We should've found a way to check in with you."

Lysandra's embrace, both fierce and comforting, conveys the depth of her worry during our absence. "A month without any sign. I couldn't help but think the worst," she admits, her voice cracking.

"Oh my gosh, Sis, I'm so sorry," I say, then chuckle, trying to lighten the mood. "Time got all wonky on us there. I totally lost track of it."

The cozy warmth of Nightshade Mansion's living room surrounds us, a comforting contrast to the icy challenge that lies before us. Miles, his face etched with a solemn resolve yet radiating reassurance, breaks the quiet that has enveloped us. "Okay, team, we're safe here for now, but let's be real—the adventure's far from finished," he begins, his voice a beacon of certainty in the swirling sea of doubts. "The Conclave of Shadows isn't just lurking in the background; it's a menacing force spreading its darkness across the stars, aiming straight for us. Sure, we're on the verge of something massive, but we're not facing it solo. We've got the Light Beings, our forebears, and the legacy left by Saturn's folks to boost us, pulling strength directly from Eridanus itself."

Lysandra, now more composed and visibly empowered by Miles' pep talk, quickly joins in. "You got it," she says, "feeling the presence of our otherworldly backers does remind us we're part of this massive, cosmic tapestry. But Miles, you're right. We need more than just spiritual oversight and the power you've been channeling. We need solid, boots-on-the-ground allies, creatures of both essence and matter, ready to join our fight."

Here, at this moment, with the fire crackling softly and shadows playing along the walls, the heft of our mission truly sinks in. Yet, amidst this solemnity, there's this unbreakable thread binding us together, a collective determination and shared vision that seems to grow stronger by the second. The spirit of my parents, those courageous souls who've handed us this legacy, seems almost tangible tonight. Their bravery and resolve fill the room, urging us to keep the balance between the forces of light and shadow.

Feeling the weight of everyone's gaze, I add, "It's easy to feel like we're just specks in the infinite vastness, facing hurdles too high to scale. But standing here with all of you, I'm filled with this unstoppable energy. Our abilities, inherited from generations of light-bringers, are not just our shield—they're our beacon, lighting the path ahead."

Miles, nodding in agreement, continues, "Protected and

steered by the Light Beings and our ancestors, powered by the legacy of Saturn's parents, their essence infuses us, lighting up hope and fortifying our resolve. But as the Conclave's plots thicken, and their shadows darken our doorstep, it's clear we need to extend our reach, to forge alliances far and wide to confront this looming threat."

Lysandra, eyes alight with enthusiasm, chimes in, "And let's not overlook the artifacts you've snagged from your journeys—the Compass, the Codex, the Crystal, and the Arcanum Celestis. They're more than just keepsakes; they're tangible proof of the forces we've harnessed and the heritage we're striving to safeguard."

"Speaking of timely reinforcements," I jump in, sensing a shift in the air, "Laila's arrival isn't just a win for our team; she symbolizes the broader call to arms. It's time to unite, to weave together allies from every corner, visible or not, in our standoff against the Conclave of Shadows."

As we lay out our battle plan, buoyed by the overwhelming support of the Light Beings, our ancestors, and my parents' undying legacy, our strategy gains an air of invincibility. With Eridanus's power pulsing through us and a steadfast commitment to amass a coalition of allies, we're ready to step into the breach, fully equipped to take on the darkness.

As the night wears on, Nightshade Mansion transforms from a mere residence to our fortress against the gathering storm. We are more than allies; we are a family bonded by a pledge of loyalty, duty, and the shared goal of shielding our world from the encroaching darkness.

Wrapping up the night, I remind everyone, "As we head off to catch some rest, let's hold onto the strength we draw from each other. This power, this unity, is what will steer us through the upcoming struggles." Facing down a daunting road, our collective spirit is unbreakable. And as Nightshade Mansion enshrouds us in its protective arms, I am imbued with an unwavering belief in our collective destiny to triumph over the shadows.

CHAPTER 8
DAWN'S FIRST LIGHT AND THE PRISM'S PROMISE

The sun's rays sneak through Nightshade Mansion's windows, painting patterns on the floor, reminding me of the intricate dance between light and shadow. The air's chill nudges me back to reality, San Francisco's fog a stark contrast to the cosmic energies we've just left behind. Lysandra, Laila, Miles, and I huddle in the kitchen, seeking warmth in the morning's quiet and the comforting aroma of brewing coffee.

"I still can't believe it was only a week," Lysandra muses, her amusement tinged with worry as she pours another cup of coffee.

Leaning against the counter, Miles catches my eye, sharing a moment of disbelief. "Time dilation wasn't in the guardian manual," he jokes, lightening the mood, but the undercurrent of tension from last night's revelations lingers.

"We need to focus," I urge, feeling the weight of our responsibilities. "The Conclave won't pause their plans for us to adjust."

Lysandra's reaction comes without hesitation, her initial worry quickly transforming into a firm resolve. "We definitely need to expand our circle of allies. It's essential we develop a strategy that encompasses a wide array of support. With the Light Beings, our ancestors, the artifacts, and the entire universe already on our side, diversifying our alliances will only strengthen our position."

Our strategy session is abruptly cut short by an unexpected interruption. The doorbell's chime stirs us from our focused deliberations, and a mixture of caution and curiosity propels us toward the door. I reach out and pull it open, finding myself face-to-face with a figure shrouded in mist.

The sunlight, bright and clear, does little to dispel the enigmatic mist that seems to weave around the visitor like a living entity. As I stand there in the open doorway, the warm day air brushes against us, infused with an unusual chill carried by the mist. It feels out of place in the daylight, as though a piece of the night has been stubbornly clinging to this figure.

Emerging from the mist as if conjured by some unseen force is Julian Blackwood, though his name has yet to be discovered. His presence, intense and wholly unanticipated, freezes us in a moment of suspended reality. His dark and searching eyes seem to pierce through the daylight's clarity, hinting at secrets and stories carried from shadows not yet dispelled by the sun.

Julian, with his muscular build sharply outlined against the bright backdrop of the day, embodies a figure both daunting and charismatic. His deep-set blue eyes, catching the sunlight, burn with an intensity that belies his unexpected visit. The mist that lingers around him clings to his dirty blonde hair, which falls to his shoulders, giving him an almost ethereal appearance. This look contrasts sharply with the streetwise sagacity etched into his features, a juxtaposition that hints at a complex history.

His unconventional and distinct attire speaks volumes about the man before us. Black Nike Air Force 1 sneakers, stark against the sunlit porch, add an unexpected twist to his ensemble, reflecting a personal style that defies the typical biker stereotype. The dark, over-dyed Levi's 501 jeans he wears, a testament to his practical yet distinctive fashion sense, complete the image of a man who defies easy categorization.

Julian Blackwood, the unexpected visitor shrouded in mist, stands before us not just as a man but as a complex amalgamation of leadership, street smarts, and a rugged charisma that is as compelling as it is unique.

"Can I help you?" My guard is up; the fine line between friend and foe is ever-present in our world.

Julian steps forward from the shadowed alcove of the front porch, his presence both commanding and enigmatic. "I believe I can be of assistance," he declares, his voice resonating with layers of hidden knowledge. "My name is Julian, Julian Blackwood, and your quest is also mine."

As we usher Julian into the living room, the remnants of our morning's tactical planning still scattered across the surfaces, he takes in the setting with a keen eye. Without waiting for us to prompt him, Julian begins to unravel his story, filling in the blanks of his sudden appearance.

"I traveled from Eldoria," he starts, his voice steady and imbued with a quiet strength. "It's a world not unlike Eridanus in its deep connection to the cosmic energies. Eldoria orbits in the same celestial neighborhood as Arcturus, closely linked to the vibrational fields that influence your own world."

He walks over to the window, peering out as if ensuring our conversation remains private. Turning back to us, his expression is both solemn and earnest. "My journey here wasn't by mere chance. In the libraries of Eldoria, among ancient scrolls and star charts, I came across prophecies and tales that led me to you. Your recent quest to Eridanus has stirred more than just the winds of fate; it has caught the attention of those who wish to tilt the cosmic scales in their favor—the Conclave of Shadows."

Miles nods at this, interjecting with a calm, informed tone. "We're well aware of the Conclave's interests and their reach, Julian, but please, continue. Your insights might shed new light on what we already know."

Encouraged, Julian resumes, his tone becoming more urgent. "I've been tracking the Conclave's movements for years, trying to predict where their dark ambitions might lead them next. When I learned of their interest in obtaining an artifact; a prism with the power to shift the balance irreversibly in their favor."

My research into arcane energies and how they're manipulated led me to the conclusion that our paths were meant to intersect.

He steps closer, his presence reassuring yet filled with a sense of urgency. "The prism they seek, is capable of refracting not just light but the very energies that bind the universe; it's more than an artifact. It's a pivot upon which future events might turn. I came here to help you secure it, to ensure that such power does not fall into the wrong hands."

Miles and I exchange a look of understanding. Julian's knowledge and his connection to the cosmic lore of Eldoria could be the key to outsmarting the Conclave. His arrival might be the edge we need to turn the tide in our favor. With renewed focus, we prepare to dive deeper into our plans, Julian's insights now guiding our next moves.

As Julian shares his knowledge, a clear strategy begins to emerge from our collective determination.

Miles and I are to embark on a quest guided by the arcane breadcrumbs Julian has laid out before us. Our mission is clear—to seek the prism, a relic of untold power and ancient majesty, believed to harness the very essence of the cosmic spectrum. This prism, shrouded in legend and cloaked in the mysteries of time, holds the potential to shift the balance in our favor, a beacon of light in the shadowed dance with our foes.

Lysandra, with her expansive network and keen strategic mind, assumes the role of our sentinel, her senses extended through the web of alliances and contacts she has nurtured over time. She is to monitor the Conclave's movements, a task as critical as it is perilous. Her vigilance becomes our shield, her intelligence our sword in the silent war waged in shadows and whispers.

Into this meticulously laid plan, Laila steps with a role uniquely her own, adding a new dimension to our collective effort. Her innate connection to the mystical and her profound understanding of the stakes involved empower her with a pivotal task. Laila is to be the bridge between the tangible and the ethereal, leveraging her unique abilities to tap into the energies and allies that dwell beyond the veil. She is tasked with harnessing the ancestral wisdom and the protective gaze of the Light Beings, ensuring that the strength and guidance of our spectral allies amplify our physical endeavors.

Laila's role transcends mere support; she is to actively engage with the energies we've tapped into on Eridanus, channeling the legacy of my parents and the ancient power of my ancestors. Her efforts are to fortify our spiritual defenses, creating a bastion of energy that shields our physical beings and enhances our endeavors. This spiritual armor, woven from the fabric of the cosmos itself, promises to be an invaluable asset in our quest for the prism and in the broader struggle against the Conclave.

As our meeting goes on into the late hours, our strategy solidifies, a multi-faceted approach to a threat that spans the breadth of the known and unknown universe. Each of us, armed with our unique abilities and roles, stands ready to partake in this intricate dance of light and shadow. Julian's wisdom, Miles and my determination, Lysandra's strategic oversight, and Laila's mystical connections form the pillars of our endeavor, a unified front against the darkness that seeks to engulf us. Together, we step forward, our paths lit by the combined might of our resolve and the celestial guardians that watch over us, ready to face whatever challenges lie ahead in our quest to secure the prism and thwart the Conclave's ominous schemes.

By the time Julian departs, promising to return at midnight, we're engulfed in a flurry of preparations. Lysandra's warning, "Be cautious with Julian. Quick trust is a luxury we can't afford," echoes my reservations. Yet, Julian's knowledge might be the key we need.

The day blurs into a frenzy of activity—brewing potions, reinforcing wards, and consecrating weapons with ancient spells. Nightshade Mansion transforms from a quiet home into a hub of anticipation and readiness.

As night draws near, tension wraps around us, a tangible force. We gather, cloaked in determination and the night's embrace, ready to embark on a journey that promises to test our limits and challenge the very essence of our mission.

Julian arrives, punctual as the night deepens, his silhouette a dark promise against the mansion's backdrop. "The path ahead is perilous," he warns, "but the balance of power hangs in the balance."

His solemn words linger as we step into the night, the mansion a silent sentinel behind us. The quest for the prism, hidden yet immensely powerful, begins under the cover of darkness, a race against time and the Conclave's dark ambitions.

Our unity becomes our greatest strength as we navigate the uncertainties ahead. Julian, a guide shrouded in mystery, leads us through the night toward a destiny intertwined with the fate of the world we vow to protect.

The journey is a testament to our resolve, a blend of strategy, magick, and the unwavering bond that ties us together. We stand on the cusp of discovery, ready to face whatever lies ahead, united by a common cause and a shared destiny.

CHAPTER 9

SHADOWS AND PRISM: A DANCE OF LIGHT AND DARK

Under the cloak of night, the city's usual vibrancy dimmed, leaving behind shadows that moved with an almost sentient grace. Our small band, led by Julian, navigated these shadows, each step a silent pact against the unseen forces conspiring beneath San Francisco's fog-laden surface. The air was heavy with the scent of damp earth and distant sea, and the sound of our footsteps echoed off the walls, a constant reminder of our presence in this hidden world.

"We're moving towards the heart of the city," Julian whispered, his voice a mere thread in the quiet. "The artifact is hidden in plain sight, shielded by ancient magicks only visible to those who know where to look."

Miles kept close, his eyes scanning the dark for any sign of a trap. "And you're sure the Conclave hasn't gotten to it first?" he asked, skepticism lacing his tone.

Before Julian could reply, he halted us with a swift, commanding gesture, steering us into the relative privacy of a narrow alley shrouded in shadows. The stark brick walls loomed over us, whispering of centuries passed. Here, away from prying eyes, he turned to face Miles's questioning gaze with an unwavering calm, his eyes glinting with a mix of determination and mystery.

Miles, ever the sentinel of our cause, regarded Julian with a mix of wariness and respect. The intensity in his gaze was mirrored only by the earnestness in his voice as he addressed our enigmatic visitor. "How do you know all of this?" he asked his question, cutting through the air with the precision of a well-honed blade. "And how did you come to have the same quest as us?" Julian's calm exterior seemed to falter for a moment, a flicker of vulnerability crossing his face before he regained his composure.

Julian, a figure shrouded in mystery, met Miles's inquiry with a calm, unwavering demeanor. His reply, when it came, was both measured and revealing. "My journey into the heart of these mysteries began long before tonight," he began, his voice carrying the weight of unspoken trials and tribulations. "Years ago, I stumbled upon fragments of an ancient prophecy hidden within the arcane texts I've dedicated my life to studying. These texts spoke of a convergence, a series of events that would threaten the very fabric of our reality."

He paused, allowing the gravity of his words to sink in before continuing. "At first, I was a skeptic, a man of logic and reason. But the more I uncovered, the more I realized that this was not mere myth. It was a call to arms, a plea from the past to those with the courage to heed it. My quest, much like yours, is not born of coincidence but of fate. We are aligned, not by chance, but by the very forces we seek to understand and protect against."

Julian's explanation, rich in detail and conviction, painted the picture of a man who had traversed the depths of ancient knowledge, his quest for understanding leading him to the same path as ours. "The threats we face, the shadows encroaching upon our world, they are but pieces of a larger puzzle. I've seen the signs, felt the shifting energies, and I've fought against the darkness in the corners where it breeds. Our missions may have begun as separate threads, but they have intertwined, guided by the same undeniable truth that now calls us to stand together."

The alley, a silent witness to our clandestine meeting, seemed to hold its breath as Julian's words hung in the air. In him, with his blend of arcane knowledge and life tested on the streets, we found not just an ally but a beacon guiding us toward a shared destiny. The weight of our mission, the gravity of the situation, was palpable in the air, and each of us felt it in our bones.

"Our fight against the Conclave isn't a simple clash of light against dark; it's a test of our will to stand together, to blend our strengths and face the oncoming storm as one," Julian concluded, his gaze locking with each of ours in turn. "Together, we're not just stronger; we're invincible."

As we step out of the alley, back into the labyrinth of the city, the night feels less oppressive, the darkness less impenetrable. Julian Blackwood, a figure shrouded in mystery, with his enigmatic stories of ancient prophecies and shared fates, has woven himself into the fabric of our mission, a reminder that in this fight, unity is not just our strength but our salvation. The road ahead may be fraught with peril, but with allies like Julian by our side, the path seems more apparent, the objective more attainable. The battle for balance continues, and together, we move forward, ready for whatever lies ahead.

The rest of our journey takes us through the city's winding streets, each turn revealing layers of history and magick intertwined; the same streets Miles and I have always loved exploring. San Francisco, with its architectural marvels and steep inclines, now reveals secrets that are more enchanting than ever before.

'We're here,' Julian announces, stopping in front of an unremarkable building nestled between towering skyscrapers. Its facade, worn by time, gives no hint of the power pulsing within. Yet, as we step inside, a world of forgotten knowledge and untold secrets unfolds before us, sparking a thrill of excitement.

"How do we get in?" I ask, peering at the locked door, no different from any other in this part of the city. "Do you have the key, Julian?"

"With this," Julian replies, producing a small, intricately carved stone from his pocket. He explains that it's a key, a relic from a forgotten era, that can unlock any door. He presses it against the door, and for a moment, nothing happens. Then, as if recognizing its master, the door clicks open, revealing darkness beyond.

Inside, the atmosphere is laden with the aroma of aged paper and the faint mustiness of dust—a library seemingly untouched by the march of time. The walls are lined with an array of ancient books and artifacts, each whispering tales of forgotten lore. The air is heavy with the weight of knowledge, and the silence is broken only by the soft rustle of pages turning in the wind.

Julian moves purposefully toward one of the library's towering shelves. His gaze fixed on a particular tome that seemed out of place amongst its dust-laden brethren—a book whose cover gleams with the lustrous sheen of silver, its beauty stark against the dim light. With a reach that bespeaks familiarity, he retrieves the book, handling it with a reverence that suggests it holds more than just printed words.

As Julian opens the silver tome, it initially appears to be nothing more than an exquisite artifact of ancient crafts-manship. However, with a deliberate motion, he passes his hand over the pages, and the room's breath seems to catch. Nestled within the heart of the book, hidden from casual view, the prism emerges. This clever concealment, a testament to the ingenuity and caution of those who sought to protect such power, reveals the prism only to those who know its secret. The anticipation and excitement in the room is palpable as we all realize the significance of this discovery.

The prism, once concealed within the book's embrace, now caught the sparse illumination, casting vibrant hues that danced and swirled with a life of their own. The spectacle of colors, alive and moving, filled the space with a sense of wonder that was almost tangible, a palpable energy that spoke to the artifact's latent power. This hidden library, with its air of ancient mystery, served as the perfect guardian for such a treasure, keeping it safe from those who would seek to misuse its capabilities until the right moment—until now.

"It's breathtaking," I whispered, my voice filled with awe and wonder.

"And dangerous," Julian added, his gaze never leaving the artifact. "The prism can bend and amplify magickal energies, but without control, it can just as easily cause destruction."

Miles inched forward, his hand trembling as it hovered inches from the artifact. "How do we use it against the Conclave?" he asked, his voice filled with a mix of fear and determination.

"That's the tricky part," Julian admitted, watching Miles's every move. "It requires a balance of energies—light and dark. Too much of one, and we risk unleashing forces we can't contain."

The room felt smaller suddenly, the weight of our task a tangible pressure against my chest. "So, what's the plan?

How do we harness its power without turning ourselves into what we're fighting against?"

Julian's eyes met mine, a spark of something unreadable within their depths. "We do it together. Balance isn't about negating the darkness but integrating it with the light. Together, we represent that balance."

Our planning was cut short by a disturbance, a ripple of energy that sent a shiver down my spine. "We're not alone," I whispered, turning towards the door just as it burst open.

Conclave coven members, their faces hidden beneath cloaks of shadow, poured into the room, their intent clear as the dark energy crackled in their palms.

The air crackled with energy as the battle erupted, a chaotic dance of light and shadow. Julian's spells weaved a protective barrier around us, each one a testament to his skill and power. Miles, his movements fluid and precise, countered each attack with a calculated ease.

Julian stood beside the prism, his focus on maintaining a shield around the artifact. "I can't hold them off and protect this," he shouted over the din of battle.

A desperate but necessary plan formed. "Use the prism," I yelled back, dodging a bolt of dark energy. Amplify our spells!"

It was a risk, the balance precarious, but our options were dwindling. Julian nodded, his hands moving over the prism in an ancient gesture. The artifact pulsed, its light expanding to envelop us.

Our combined powers, amplified by the prism, created

a vortex of energy that swept through the room. The Conclave agents, caught in the torrent, were swept away, their dark magick dissipating like smoke in the wind.

As the last of them vanished, the room fell silent; the only sound was our ragged breathing. The prism, once a beacon of swirling colors, dimmed, its light extinguished as if it never was.

"We did it," Miles said, the relief palpable in his voice.

"We did," I agreed, my gaze on the now inert prism. "But at what cost?"

Julian picked up the artifact and examined it closely. "The prism's magick is spent, at least for now. It saved us, but it's a temporary victory. The Conclave of Shadows will come again."

Our eyes met, a silent agreement passing between us. This battle may be over, but the war raged on. We had the prism, a tool of immense power, but its true potential, its role in the balance we sought to protect, remained a mystery.

"We'll figure it out," I announced with newfound determination. "Together, we'll unlock this prism's true potential and continue our fight for balance and light."

As we left the hidden library, the city of San Francisco awaited, its secrets and shadows a backdrop to our ongoing fight. The prism, now in our possession, was both a promise and a warning—a reminder that the battle for balance was never truly over.

And as the sun rose, casting the first light of dawn over

the city, I knew that whatever came next, we would face it together, our bonds strengthened by the battles we had fought and the victories we had won. The road ahead was uncertain, but our resolve was unwavering. We were guardians, protectors of the light, and defenders of balance. The journey continued, and we were ready.

CHAPTER 10

DAWN'S REVELATIONS AND UNSEEN DANGERS

As dawn's light spills into Nightshade Mansion, cleansing the darkness of night, it brings little solace to the unrest that lies within. The aftermath of our skirmish over the prism has left a palpable tension hanging in the air, a silent witness to the battle fought and the challenges yet to come. It's within these hallowed walls, amidst the lingering shadows, that Laila finds us, her presence a soothing balm to our weary souls.

Laila, a figure of ethereal grace, stands as a beacon of peace amidst the chaos that has consumed our lives. Her voice, a soothing melody, fills the room, binding us in a collective embrace of warmth and determination. "Your courage has not gone unnoticed," she begins, her words carrying a weight of wisdom. "Yet, the path ahead holds dangers yet unseen."

Her gaze, imbued with centuries of guardianship, locks

with mine, and I'm reminded of the depth of her vow to protect, a promise made amidst the joy of my wedding, now a beacon in the storm of our quest.

Miles, his voice laced with a skeptic's caution, challenges Laila's vague premonitions. "We've dealt a blow to the Conclave, what more shadows could possibly lurk beyond their reach?" His words hang in the air, a testament to the doubt that lingers.

Laila's response, tinged with sorrow, carries a weight that shrouds the room in silence. "The Conclave's ambitions have stirred ancient forces, beings that have slumbered until now, awakened by the prism's misuse. Their intentions, their powers, remain a mystery."

A chill descends, her words casting a pall over us. Julian, until now a quiet observer, shifts, unease etched into his features. "The ripples we've sent through the realms are not without consequence. The prism's power was never meant for such recklessness."

Rising to confront the reality of our actions, I demand clarity. "What must we do? How do we brace against threats we cannot foresee?"

Laila, her grace, a shield against despair, offers a path forward. "We fortify our defenses, we seek knowledge, and we confront these threats as one." Her touch, light upon my hand, is a lifeline to her promise of unwavering support.

Lysandra's pragmatic voice cuts through the gathering dread. "We need insights into these hidden dangers. Understanding them is key to our defense."

Agreement unites us. Laila vows to use her deep connections to the natural and mystical realms for answers, while Julian pledges to scour the annals of arcane lore for clues hidden within the prism's storied past.

As the others disperse, Laila's solemn words draw me aside. "There's more you should know, concerning Daniel's intentions and the secrets he guards."

Her revelation sends waves of shock through me. "What secrets?" I whisper, fear and disbelief mingling in my voice.

"Not here," she insists, leading me to the sanctuary of the mansion's gardens, where the world seems untouched by the shadows of our discussions.

Amidst the tranquil beauty of dawn-kissed flora, Laila unveils a truth that fractures the ground beneath me. "Daniel's motives are intertwined with the Conclave more deeply than mere alliance. His pursuit of the prism is driven by a desire for power, not protection."

Reeling from her words, I grapple with the betrayal. "But why? How?"

Laila's steady presence offers a semblance of strength. "His reasons are his own, yet not all hope is lost. The path is perilous, but together, we shall navigate its dangers."

Returning to the mansion, now bathed in the whole light of day, I carry the weight of her revelations. Yet, I am bolstered by the knowledge that no matter the trials we face, we do so together, bound by a resilience that no shadow can diminish.

CHAPTER II

ALLIANCE WITH THE ELEMENTAL GUARDIANS

The first light of dawn bathes Nightshade Mansion in a warm glow, a stark contrast to the gravity of our urgent mission today. We are to swiftly seek out the Elemental Guardians, ancient protectors whose wisdom and power might be our only hope against the encroaching darkness Laila and Julian have warned us about.

In the library, where the scent of aged paper mingles with the weight of countless histories, we stand united: Miles, a battle-hardened warrior with a strategic mind that shapes every move; Lysandra, a learned scholar who deciphers ancient symbols and magick with ease; Laila, a serene yet imposing figure, deeply attuned to the Elemental Guardians; and me, Saturn, a descendant of a powerful legacy. My mission isn't about proving my worth but about fulfilling my purpose—to protect Earth and the universe itself. The air vibrates with anticipation, charged with the gravity of our impending journey that casts a long shadow over our hearts.

"We're headed into the unknown," Lysandra says, breaking the silence as her fingers trace ancient symbols on the map. Her voice, usually full of confidence, wavers slightly under the weight of our task.

"But we'll do it together, united in our purpose," I add, trying to keep my voice steady despite the anxious flutter in my stomach.

Laila, always calm but firm, nods. "The Elemental Guardians have kept Earth's balance for ages, but they've stayed out of human conflicts. Convincing them to help us… well, that's a challenge no one's dared to tackle."

"How do we get beings as old as time to join us?" Miles wonders aloud, his strategic mind already puzzling through the enormity of what we're asking.

"It's not about convincing them," Laila says with certainty, "but sharing a vision of balance. The disturbances we've seen, the misuse of the prism—they affect everyone, not just humans."

Emboldened by Laila's insight, we head out at dawn. The city stirs around us, oblivious to the secret battles lurking in its shadows. We make our way through crowded streets, past markets, and intersections until the hum of civilization fades away. Our path leads into a realm where ancient magick still thrives, untouched by the relentless march of modern life.

The dense forest wraps around us like a living entity, a lush world that stretches beyond what we can see. Towering trees form a canopy that filters the sunlight into glowing beams, casting the forest floor in twilight. Moss and ferns cover the ground, and the air is rich with the scent of Earth and wood. Birdsong, rustling leaves, and the soft murmur of a nearby stream create a symphony of life that stirs our souls.

As we venture deeper, the forest seems to watch us—an ancient guardian hidden in the shadows, protecting this sacred ground. Laila leads us to a clearing that feels alive with the wild energy of the forest. A natural cathedral, where light and shadow create an otherworldly mosaic on the ground, towers above us with branches reaching skyward. At its center stands a weathered stone altar etched with symbols representing fire, water, Earth, and air—the very elements that hold everything together.

Laila raises her arms, her posture radiating power and reverence. Her voice breaks the silence like a hymn, rippling through the air thick with ancient magick. Her invocation is a call and a plea woven with the language of Earth and sky, water and fire.

"Guardians of the ancient wilds, hear my call," she says, her voice unwavering. "Elements that dance in the eternal cycle, I summon you to this sacred circle. From the depths of the Earth to the endless skies, from roaring flames to flowing waters, lend us your strength, wisdom, and essence."

She continues, "Earth, solid and enduring, grant us your resilience. Let the ground beneath us be a firm foundation. Air, bringer of breath and change, guide us with clarity and vision."

After a deep breath, she speaks from the world's soul, "FireFire, wild and untamed, ignite our courage and willpower. Water, ever flowing, wash away our doubts, heal our wounds, and share your wisdom."

She crescendos, "To the spirits of the north, south, east, and west, join us on this path. Protect us, guide us, and lend us your energy."

When she finishes, the air pulses with a primal power. The ground hums in harmony with Laila's words, connecting her plea to the very heartbeat of the world. The forest blurs the lines between the seen and unseen, and the elemental forces awaken, drawn to her sincerity. The Guardians materialize, each embodying their elements: fire, water, Earth, and air. They stand like masterpieces of natural power, reminding us of the potent forces that keep life in balance.

We stand in awe, barely breathing, as we witness these ancient beings appear. Their majesty is beyond words—it is a rare moment when time pauses, and we see the beauty of the natural world.

"We come seeking your help," Laila's voice rings out. "The balance you protect is in danger from forces that could destroy the very fabric of existence."

Their deliberation is silent but intense, a council

deciding our fate. The firewire Guardian, a being of flame, finally asks, "Why should we, who have watched epochs pass, intervene in the affairs of mortals?"

With the invocation hanging in the air, I step forward, not as a human but as Saturn, an immortal star seed witch. I'm woven from the cosmic fabric of the universe. "We're not just mortals. We are star seed witches, our souls lit by the stars themselves," I declare, my voice ringing with ancient melodies. "We're driven to confront the shadows and uphold the balance that nourishes life."

I share our journey and trials, the obstacles we've faced, and how we've grown stronger with every challenge. "We're brave, resilient, and dedicated to protecting balance across the cosmos."

I pause to let the truth sink in. "Our quest mirrors your ancient duty. Our paths are entwined, our destinies linked. We're connected by a shared commitment to keep the harmony that sustains everything."

In this forest clearing, I sense a connection between us. "We're eternal like you. Together, our combined power can push back the darkness and protect the cosmic balance."

The silence that follows is charged, and there's a shift in the air—a cosmic alignment. The Guardians promise their aid. "We'll stand with you," says the water Guardian, a voice like a river. "For the threat you face touches us all."

Their promise lights up our darkest hour. As we leave the forest, the Guardians whisper through the trees, and we walk with newfound strength.

Our return is quiet, each of us reflecting on the road ahead. Nightshade Mansion looms into view, a reminder of the world we fight to protect. "With the Guardians' help, we stand a chance," I say, voicing our shared hope.

We step over the threshold, fortified by new alliances and a shared resolve to protect the balance of our world.

And in that moment, as we gear up for the trials ahead, I know we'll face whatever challenges come our way—as united guardians of the light, ready to defend against the shadows.

CHAPTER 12

ALLIANCE FROM THE COSMOS

A week has passed since our alliance with the Elemental Guardians, and the power and confidence they've instilled in us resonate deeply. Still, the complexity of our mission against the Conclave continues to unravel in ways we couldn't have foreseen. As usual, we're gathered in Nightshade Mansion's spacious living room, the heart of our strategic operations where ancient magick and modern determination meet.

Miles, Lysandra, Julian, Laila, and I are engrossed in discussion, our focus laser-sharp on predicting the Conclave's next moves and the elusive shadowy threats. The weight of responsibility presses down on us, but the crackling fire in the hearth and the comforting surroundings of the mansion offer a little solace.

The intense conversation is interrupted by the jarring chime of the doorbell—a sound so unusual in the secluded sanctuary that it snaps us out of our focus. We exchange puzzled glances, our curiosity piqued by this unexpected intrusion.

"I'll get it," I say, rising from the plush armchair. The mansion's corridors feel charged with anticipation as I make my way to the door. With each step, my sense of expectation builds. When I open the door, I'm met with a sight that's as surprising as it is intriguing.

Standing before me are three individuals, each radiating a unique energy that echoes the cosmos itself. Orion Vega, Valerie Storm, and Samantha Wilde introduce themselves, their presence like a testament to how the universe aligns allies to our cause.

Orion's gaze, deep and reflective as the night sky, meets mine. "We've been called by the universe itself," he says, his voice carrying the weight of distant stars. "We've been guided to this place to offer our aid against the darkness that threatens to consume."

Valerie, her eyes glowing with the power of the storms she commands, nods firmly. "Our abilities, our very essence, are at your disposal. The elements of weather heed my call, and I'm ready to wield them in our collective struggle."

Samantha, her aura radiating the serene power of the earth, offers a warm smile. "And I, connected to the heartbeat of the natural world, bring my understanding and command of nature to strengthen our defenses and heal our wounds."

Their arrival and willingness to join our cause stir a whirlwind of emotions. We eagerly usher them into the living room, making introductions amid a mix of surprise, excitement, and a hint of relief.

"This is incredible," Lysandra muses, her strategic mind already weighing the possibilities. "Your abilities could significantly shift how we approach confronting the Conclave."

Miles, ever the tactician, leans forward, intrigued. "Orion, can your foresight give us specifics on the Conclave's next move?"

Orion's response is thoughtful and measured. "The cosmos grants visions, not certainties. But I can sense the ripples of their intentions, which might guide our strategy."

"And Valerie," Laila interjects with curiosity, "how precise is your control over the elements? Could you, for instance, direct a storm specifically at the Conclave's forces?"

"With enough focus and the right conditions, yes," Valerie asserts confidently. "The weather is a powerful ally, and I've honed my abilities to command it precisely."

Samantha's contribution is no less impressive. "And I can make sure the land itself aids us, offering sanctuary or creating a barrier against those who seek to harm."

The dynamics of our gathering shift with Orion, Valerie, and Samantha in the room. Their arrival, seemingly orchestrated by the cosmos, brings new strength to our ranks and rekindles hope.

"Our mission grows more complex, but so does our arsenal," Julian notes, recognizing the potential of our expanded team.

Integrating our new allies into our planning makes the mansion feel less like a fortress against the dark and more like a beacon of light, drawing together those destined to stand against the shadows. The universe is weaving our destinies together in this fight for balance and harmony.

As the night wears on and our discussions deepen, strategies form, and bonds strengthen. I can't help but feel that this unexpected convergence of souls and powers marks a turning point in our battle against the Conclave. The path ahead remains treacherous, but with Orion, Valerie, and Samantha at our side, we're better equipped than ever to face whatever lurks in the shadows.

CHAPTER 13

SHADOWS WITHIN AND BEYOND

Training, strategizing, and putting on a magick showcase—it's been a circus of power and flair as we've worked to fold our new allies into the mix. With the Nightshade Mansion cloaked in night and wrapped in mystery, our newfound bond with the Elemental Guardians, those beings of fire, water, earth, and air, gives us the confidence to take on anything. But Julian's ominous hints about unseen threats loom over us like a fog nobody wants to walk through.

We're gathered in the study, surrounded by the comforting glow of the fireplace and ancient tomes packed with wisdom, forming a council of fate-bound allies— Miles, Lysandra, Laila, Orion, Valerie, and Samantha. We're here to unravel the complexities of our mission to protect the world from the Conclave's meddling with magick. The air smells like old leather and wood smoke, humming with tension.

Julian bursts in, piercing the quiet of our strategizing like a sledgehammer to a delicate vase. "The Conclave of Shadows knows about our alliance with the Guardians," he announces, his grave tone giving weight to his words like a theatrical villain delivering foreboding news.

Miles furrows his brow like he's determined to iron it flat and immediately challenges Julian's claim. "How do you know that?" His suspicion wafts across the room like a cloud of smoke.

Julian, caught in the spotlight, carefully crafts his response, trying to keep the attention off himself. "I intercepted a message meant for the Conclave. There's a breach among us, but it's not from those you'd expect." He leaves just enough ambiguity to make everyone uneasy without revealing anything specific.

The room's atmosphere shifts as suspicion snakes through the air, and we glance at one another with a hint of doubt. Orion steps forward, confidence etched into his stance. "My loyalty is with the stars and this cause. My visions guided me here to stand against darkness, not betray it."

Valerie, calm as the stillness before the storm, adds, "I command the tempests to protect, not to tear us apart. My power is yours, unequivocally. Betrayal serves me no purpose."

Samantha, serene but firm, nods. "My harmony with

the earth and its creatures is central to who I am. Betraying this cause would be betraying myself, and that's not my style."

Their declarations fill the study, each resolute in loyalty. But Julian's insinuation has planted seeds of doubt, like a lingering aftertaste.

Lysandra, ever the voice of reason, steps up. "We must not let suspicion divide us. Our strength lies in unity and trust."

Laila echoes that. "This uncertainty is what the Conclave desires. Let's focus on the real enemy, not shadows among us."

Feeling the weight of leadership, I propose, "Let's reinforce our defenses and our trust in one another. If there is a traitor among us, we will uncover them through unity, not division."

Julian stands quietly to the side, seemingly content that his vague hints have sown a little discord. We can't figure out what his angle is, but we know he's trying to stir the pot.

As the meeting disperses, the unease lingers like a cloud of doubt—a reminder of the challenges we face not just from the Conclave but also from within our ranks. But even through these whispers of suspicion, our commitment to the cause and each other remains unshaken. After all, we're united, even if Julian keeps dropping ominous prophecies like breadcrumbs to confusion.

CHAPTER 14
REVELATIONS ABOVE THE SQUARE

Training, strategizing, and putting on a magick showcase—it's been a circus Of power and flair as we've worked to fold our new allies into the mix. With the Nightshade Mansion cloaked in night and wrapped in mystery, our newfound bond with the Elemental Guardians, those beings of fire, water, earth, and air, gives us the confidence to take on anything. But Julian's ominous hints about unseen threats loom over us like a fog nobody wants to walk through.

We're gathered in the study, surrounded by the comforting glow of the fireplace and ancient tomes packed with wisdom, forming a council of fate-bound allies—Miles, Lysandra, Laila, Orion, Valerie, and Samantha. We're here to unravel the complexities of our mission to protect the world from the Conclave's meddling with magick. The air smells like old leather and wood smoke, humming with tension.

Julian bursts in, piercing the quiet of our strategizing like a sledgehammer to a delicate vase. "The Conclave of Shadows knows about our alliance with the Guardians," he announces, his grave tone giving weight to his words like a theatrical villain delivering foreboding news.

Miles furrows his brow like he's determined to iron it flat and immediately challenges Julian's claim. "How do you know that?" His suspicion wafts across the room like a cloud of smoke.

Julian, caught in the spotlight, gives a carefully crafted response, trying to keep the attention off himself. "I intercepted a message meant for the Conclave. There's a breach among us, but it's not from those you'd expect." He leaves just enough ambiguity to make everyone uneasy without revealing anything specific.

The room's atmosphere shifts as suspicion snakes through the air, and we glance at one another with a hint of doubt. Orion steps forward, confidence etched into his stance. "My loyalty is with the stars and this cause. My visions guided me here to stand against darkness, not betray it."

Valerie, calm as the stillness before the storm, adds, "I command the tempests to protect, not to tear us apart. My power is yours, unequivocally. Betrayal serves me no purpose."

Samantha, serene but firm, nods. "My harmony with

the earth and its creatures is central to who I am. Betraying this cause would be betraying myself, and that's not my style."

Their declarations fill the study, each one resolute in loyalty. But Julian's insinuation has planted seeds of doubt, like a nagging aftertaste that lingers.

Lysandra, ever the voice of reason, steps up. "We must not let suspicion divide us. Our strength lies in unity and trust."

Laila echoes that. "This uncertainty is what the Conclave desires. Let's focus on the real enemy, not shadows among us."

Feeling the weight of leadership, I propose, "Let's reinforce our defenses and our trust in one another. If there is a traitor among us, we will uncover them through unity, not division."

Julian stands quietly to the side, seemingly content that his vague hints have sown a little discord. We can't figure out what his angle is, but we know he's trying to stir the pot.

As the meeting disperses, the unease lingers like a cloud of doubt—a reminder of the challenges we face not just from the Conclave but also from within our ranks. But even through these whispers of suspicion, our commitment to the cause and each other remains unshaken. After all, we're united, even if Julian keeps dropping ominous prophecies like breadcrumbs to confusion.

CHAPTER 15
UNVEILING SHADOWS

As the new day dawns, soft light filters through the windows of Nightshade Mansion, but the morning's calm is overshadowed by the unrest lingering from our last gathering. This refuge now stands as a bulwark on the edge of conflict, its halls filled with doubt and anticipation.

Miles breaks the silence with a call to action. "We can't let fear or suspicion stymie us. If the Conclave knows about our alliance with the Elemental Guardians, they'll act fast. We've got to get ahead of them."

Lysandra, weary but resolved from a night of poring over arcane texts, agrees. "Julian's misdirection strategy has merit. If we lead the Conclave to believe we're headed in the wrong direction, we can unveil their real intentions."

Laila, standing by the window, adds in her calm yet compelling voice, "The Earth itself feels the strain of this imbalance. The Guardians' involvement shows how severe the threat is. We need to decipher the Conclave's movements and understand the dangers Julian warned us about."

Amid these discussions, I voice the concern weighing heavily on all our minds. "What about the betrayer among us? How do we deal with someone who could sabotage us from within?"

Julian steps forward, his tone steady and composed. "We proceed with caution but without fear. Our coordinated actions will reveal the traitor in time. For now, we should focus on the bigger threat."

Our plan unfolds like a mosaic of deception, aiming to outmaneuver our unseen adversary. Miles and Lysandra orchestrate diversions to mislead the Conclave while Laila, Julian, and I delve deeper into the lurking threats to find insights that could tip the balance in our favor.

The city stretches out below us as we venture forth, its alleys and shadows playing silent host to unseen conflict. Our path takes us beneath the surface into the forgotten catacombs where ancient magick lies dormant.

Laila's attunement to natural forces leads us through the maze, her manipulation of light revealing hidden runes and passages. The catacombs whisper long-buried secrets, and the air is thick with the musk of damp earth and echoes from forgotten ages.

We discover the first clue—runes etched into the stone that describe an ancient covenant binding the Elemental Guardians to Earth itself.

"These aren't just historical records," Julian says, tracing the carvings with reverent fingers. "They're a warning. This covenant was made to maintain balance but also includes a way to summon the Guardians if the world's equilibrium is ever threatened."

The discovery gives our mission newfound urgency. If the Conclave's schemes can tip the scales, we may need to call upon the Guardians' complete power to prevent catastrophe.

As we advance, the feeling of being watched intensifies, growing with every step deeper into the labyrinth. The air smells of damp earth, and our footsteps echo through the tunnels, adding to the sense of isolation and danger.

The threat materializes quickly as shadows morph into assailants—the Conclave's agents, wielding spells of entrapment and destruction.

The battle that follows is a clash of magick and strategy. Laila illuminates the darkness with her mastery over the elements, scattering enemies with raw elemental force. Julian counters their magick with precise arcane energy, turning their spells against them and shifting the fight in our favor.

When the dust settles, silence returns to the catacombs, but the message is clear: we're targets in a game of dark ambitions.

"We need to move faster," I assert, the battle sharpening my resolve. "These catacomb secrets are vital, and the Conclave's desperation shows their value."

We press on, unraveling a narrative that binds the Guardians to Earth's fate. Every discovery brings us closer to understanding the Conclave's true intentions and how the Elemental Guardians can help protect the world.

As we emerge from the catacombs into the early light of dawn, we realize time is a luxury we can't afford. The Conclave's threat and the shadow of betrayal are just the beginning of our trials. But with the lore we've uncovered and the alliances we've built, we're resolute.

The battle for balance and the very essence of our world is unfolding, and we're at the heart of it—a united front against the approaching void. Despite the darkness around us, our unity is our strength. We're not just fighting for survival; we're fighting for the soul of our world.

CHAPTER 16

UNEARTHING THE HEARTHSTONE

The early afternoon light filters through the curtains of Nightshade Mansion, casting a warm, inviting glow over the kitchen. The air is rich with the aroma of freshly brewed coffee, a comforting presence amid the whirlwind of our recent discoveries. Still, the looming threat of the Conclave of Shadows, like a storm on the horizon, adds a palpable tension to the calm of the midday.

"How's everyone holding up?" I inquire, scanning the faces of my friends and allies. It's a simple question aimed at easing the weight of our shared worries amidst the day's daunting agenda.

"We're managing, Saturn," Lysandra responds, her attention momentarily shifting from the ancient texts spread before her. "The revelation about the hearthstone has certainly provided us with a new direction."

Ah, the hearthstone. Its very existence, a secret concealed within the ancient pages of the Eridanus Book of Shadows, was a mystery to us until just days ago. Its discovery, shrouded in enigma, has been nothing short of transformative.

"Let's not forget how we stumbled upon this information," Julian adds, leaning against the counter with a contemplative look. "It was the Eridanus Book of Shadows that led us to the hearthstone, thanks to Saturn's ability to unlock its secrets."

Miles nods, his gaze filled with pride and awe. 'Indeed. It was the perfect fusion of Saturn's unique heritage and the Book's ancient knowledge that guided us here. The hearthstone isn't merely a legend; it's a tangible beacon of hope.'

The Eridanus Book of Shadows, an ancient tome passed down through my family, has always been a source of mystery and power. Its pages hold secrets that can shape destinies and unlock the mysteries of the universe. Yet, I could never have anticipated it leading us to something as monumental as the hearthstone—a gem infused with the Earth's raw elemental essence, capable of restoring balance to a world on the brink of darkness.

Laila places a reassuring hand on my shoulder. "Your connection to the hearthstone, Saturn, it's more than fate. It's a reflection of the balance you embody, especially now," she says, casting a meaningful glance at my swollen belly.

"You and the child you carry are key to awakening the hearthstone's power."

The weight of responsibility settles over me like a cloak, both heavy and invigorating. The Hearthstone's potential, safeguarded by the ancient knowledge of the Eridanus Book of Shadows, represents a beacon of light in our struggle against the Conclave. This fight isn't just for the present—it's for the future, one that my child will inherit.

"We must approach this with utmost care," Miles asserts, breaking into my thoughts. "The Conclave will stop at nothing to prevent us from harnessing the hearthstone's power."

"Our plan must be flawless," Lysandra adds, focused on maps and notes. "Every precaution is necessary to ensure our journey to the Ancestral Forest, where the hearthstone resides, is safe and successful."

Julian, always the strategist, suggests additional protective measures. "We'll need wards strong enough to shield us from the Conclave's prying eyes. I'll ensure our tracks are covered."

As the day progresses, Nightshade Mansion hums with purposeful activity. We're not just a team; we're a united front, each of us playing a vital role in the mission that lies ahead. The Eridanus Book of Shadows, once a keeper of our family's secrets, now guides us toward a power that could shift the tides of our battle.

As I prepare for the journey that awaits us, I steal a moment of solitude in the soon-to-be nursery, surrounded by visions of the future. The hearthstone, with its promise of equilibrium and rejuvenation, feels like the first stride toward a world where light triumphs over darkness. The path we're about to tread is arduous, but with the unwavering support of my comrades and the sagacity of the Eridanus Book of Shadows, I'm prepared.

Tomorrow, we embark on a journey to unlock the hearthstone's enigmas, not just for ourselves but for all who will follow in our footsteps. It's a mission that was birthed in the past, carried in the present, and destined to sculpt the future. Together, we stride into the uncharted, our hearts brimming with hope and our minds steadfast on triumph.

CHAPTER 17

THE QUEST FOR THE HEARTHSTONE

When we gather at the entrance of Nightshade Mansion, the first light of dawn hasn't yet kissed the horizon, and our silhouettes are barely distinguishable in the predawn gloom. The air is thick with anticipation and the crisp promise of an autumn morning. Today, we embark on our quest for the hearthstone, armed with hope and the secrets unlocked by the Eridanus Book of Shadows.

"I didn't think I'd ever be up this early without complaining," Miles mutters, his breath visible in the cool air as he loads the last of our gear into the vehicle. His voice holds a mix of exhaustion and excitement, a testament to his commitment to our cause.

"It's the promise of adventure and the allure of magick," Lysandra replies, her voice steady despite the long night. "Besides, the hearthstone isn't going to find itself."

Then, she casts a teasing glance at Miles, adding with a smirk, "You might as well get used to waking up early because once the baby comes, you'll have no choice!"

Her words, delivered with playful mischief, lighten the mood and remind us all of the shared sense of purpose that brought us together, even if it means trading a little sleep for the magick that lies ahead.

Laila, a petite woman with a warm smile and a twinkle in her eyes, ever the nurturer, hands me a flask filled with a warm, herbal concoction. 'For strength and warmth,' she says, smiling. 'We'll need both where we're headed.' Her voice, soft and comforting, is a balm to our nerves.

Julian checks his watch, then nods to us. 'We should leave now to avoid any prying eyes. The Conclave, seeking to control the hearthstone's power, may not know our exact plans, but they're always watching, ready to strike if they sense a threat to their dominance.'

The drive to the Ancestral Forest is quiet, the roads empty as the world around us slowly awakens. Each of us is lost in thought as we contemplate the significance of our mission. The hearthstone, a relic of immense power and the key to restoring balance in our world represents more than a tactical advantage—it's a symbol of the harmony we seek to bring back.

As we approach the forest, the first rays of sunlight filter through the dense canopy, creating patterns of light and shadow that dance across the forest floor. The air here is alive, pulsing with ancient magick and the whispered secrets of the Earth. The scent of damp Earth and decaying leaves fills our nostrils, and the distant chirping of birds and rustling of leaves is a constant reminder of the forest's vibrant life.

"We're close," I announce, feeling a pull in my core, a guiding force that leads us deeper into the heart of the forest. "The hearthstone calls."

Miles parks the vehicle, and we proceed on foot, the forest welcoming us with open arms. The connection I feel to this place deepens with every step, a reminder of the ties that bind me to the Eridanus legacy and the life I carry within.

"The Eridanus Book of Shadows mentioned guardians," Julian says, his voice low as we navigate the underbrush. "Be on your guard."

We advance cautiously, aware of the weight of our quest and the eyes of unseen protectors upon us. The deeper we go, the more vibrant the forest becomes; its magick is almost tangible.

After what feels like hours, we arrive at a clearing bathed in sunlight; at its center, a pedestal of ancient stone cradling the hearthstone. The gem glows softly, its energy harmonious and inviting.

"It's beautiful," Laila breathes, her awe echoing my sentiments.

Lysandra steps forward, her gaze fixed intently on the hearthstone. "Saturn, it's waiting for you."

I approach the pedestal with a deep breath, my hands

trembling slightly as I reach out. The moment my fingers brush the hearthstone's surface, warmth surges through me, an ancient and profound connection. The stone's energy resonates with my own like an old friend, and I know this is the moment we've all been waiting for.

The air hums around us, and the forest itself seems to hold its breath as the hearthstone's glow intensifies, bathing everything in ethereal light. I close my eyes, allowing the energy to flow through me, intertwining with my own and the new life growing within.

With the words coming from my heart, I begin the enchantment, my voice steady and sure. "Oh mighty hearthstone, bearer of ancient wisdom and energy eternal, merge your light with mine. Grant me the power of balance and harmony, so I may wield your strength to guide our world."

The stone pulses with energy, its warm light spilling out and enveloping me in its embrace. My hands rest on its surface as a torrent of energy rushes through my veins, connecting with my core. I feel it in every fiber of my being —a surge that fills my mind with clarity and my spirit with purpose.

The spell reaches its crescendo, and the energy finally stabilizes, settling deep within me like an ember burning softly. I open my eyes to find the world around me sharper, more alive. The hearthstone, now dim but still radiantly beautiful, remains a testament to balance and harmony.

"You did it," Miles says, relief and pride in his voice.

"Yeah," I reply softly, my fingers tracing the stone's excellent surface one last time. "We really did."

I turn to see the team smiling back at me, each of them carrying a glimmer of hope in their eyes. We've harnessed a force of unimaginable power, and together, we'll wield it to safeguard the world we love.

"We should head back," Julian suggests, ever mindful of potential threats. "The Conclave won't be far behind."

Our return to Nightshade Mansion is swift. The hearthstone is secured among our belongings, its presence a beacon of hope. As we cross the threshold of the mansion, the weight of our journey lifts, replaced by a sense of accomplishment and the promise of challenges yet to come.

"We've taken the first step," I tell my companions, my heart brimming with gratitude and resolve. "Together, we'll tackle whatever lies ahead, united in our cause and strengthened by our bonds."

In the safety of Nightshade Mansion, with the hearthstone now ours, we're one step closer to restoring balance. The journey has been extended, and the path forward remains uncertain, but for now, we celebrate our victory. The quest for the Hearthstone may be over, but our fight continues. Together, we're ready for the next chapter, whatever it brings. As the sun sets on this stage of our journey, we know the real adventure is just beginning.

CHAPTER 18
BETRAYAL UNVEILED

The morning sun spills over Nightshade Mansion, casting long shadows across the garden. It's been two months since we retrieved the hearthstone, a crucial beacon in our ongoing battle with the Conclave. But now, tension sizzles among us like a fuse waiting to ignite. There's a traitor in our ranks, and no one knows who.

Over breakfast, Saturn and I exchange a look, her resilience glowing even in her pregnancy. "How're you holding up?" I ask, echoing Lysandra's question from earlier. My tone blends concern with unwavering determination.

"Both the baby and I are strong, ready for whatever today reveals," she replies, her hand cradling her belly protectively, her spirit as bright as ever.

Orion, Valerie, and Samantha sit across from us, their

unwavering commitment lending strength to our group. "We're in this together, no matter what," Orion says firmly, his voice brimming with determination.

"Absolutely," Valerie agrees. "The Conclave won't know what hit them."

Samantha nods solemnly. "Nature's on our side, and the Conclave's got another thing coming if they think we'll let them tear everything apart."

Laila's entrance adds a note of calm to the air. "The Earth tells tales of turmoil but whispers hope," she says, grounding us with her steady presence. "We're not alone."

"The Conclave is biding their time, waiting for us to stumble," Lysandra adds, her strategic insight slicing through the uncertainty. "We need to shore up our defenses."

In the serene embrace of the mansion's garden, where nature's tranquility contrasts with the weight of our gathering, Julian steps forward, bringing a chilling revelation.

"The prism," he begins, his voice heavy with secrets untold, "is the Conclave's key to unleashing chaos not seen since the fall of Atlantis. They want to harness its power to disrupt the elemental balance, threatening not just Eridanus but Earth itself."

Saturn and I share a knowing glance, memories of Thalios's detailed account of Atlantis's demise flooding back. The parallels between Atlantis's fate and what awaits us if the Conclave succeeds are unsettling.

Unaware of our silent exchange, Julian continues, "The

prism can control the elements, and in the Conclave's hands, it's a weapon of unimaginable destruction. The fall of Atlantis was just a precursor to their ambitions. They want to tear down and rebuild the cosmic order to suit them."

His words settle like lead in the air. I decide to expose the darkness within us. "It's always so curious, Julian, how intimately you know the Conclave's intentions," I interject, letting my suspicion bleed through. "I took the liberty of enhancing your wards to reveal any traitor. And they just lit up."

The shock ripples through the group like a stone cast into a still pond. "Julian, how could you?" Lysandra's voice cuts through the tension.

Julian, caught in the snare of his deceit, tries to mask his shock with indignation. "This is a mistake. You're misreading the wards!"

I lay out my modifications. "I infused them with a revealing spell, intertwining truth-seeking magick with the original wards. They were designed to resonate in the presence of betrayal, and resonate they did, Julian. Right at you."

The realization dawns, irrefutable and damning. Laila's disappointment is palpable. "You were our ally, Julian. How could you betray everything we've fought for?"

His facade crumbles as he attempts to justify his actions. "The Conclave... they promised me power and family loyalty. I've been alone my whole life, and belonging to the Conclave of Shadows seemed like a dream."

The air thickens with betrayal. Saturn, ever the heart of our group, asks the question on everyone's mind, "What do we do with him?"

After a heavy silence, we agree. "Keep him captive," I declare, the weight of leadership pressing down on me. "Until this fight is over. He's too dangerous to leave unchecked, but his knowledge could be valuable."

Orion, Valerie, and Samantha stand resolute beside me as Julian is led away, the trust he once held shattered into dust. As the group disperses, a somber resolve settles over us. The battle lines are drawn clearer now, with the prism's power and the betrayal in our ranks exposed.

The coming days promise a showdown of epic proportions, with the fate of Eridanus, Earth, and the universe hanging in the balance. Our resolve will be tested, but our unity burns brighter against the dark. For the world we protect and the future we dream of, we stand ready, guardians against the night, with dawn's promise guiding our way.

CHAPTER 19
THE EVE OF THE BATTLE

When we gather in the main hall of Nightshade Mansion, the morning sun has barely begun its ascent. Today marks not just another day in our prolonged struggle against the Conclave but the eve of what feels like an inevitable confrontation. The revelation of Julian's betrayal, a wound still fresh and raw, hangs heavily over us, a palpable reminder of the betrayal that had been lurking within our ranks.

As I survey the room, I am struck by the unwavering determination etched on every face. Saturn, her pregnancy now visible, stands with a resilience that defies her condition, her hand protectively cradling her belly. Lysandra, deep in her study of maps and scrolls, furrows her brow in concentration. Meanwhile, Laila engages in a calm conversation with our allies, Orion, Valerie, and Samantha, each of whom brings a unique strength to our cause.

"We can't let Julian's betrayal distract us from the task at hand," I begin, breaking the heavy silence. "The Conclave won't wait for us to regroup. We need to be proactive."

Saturn nods in agreement, her gaze meeting mine. "We've come too far to let their darkness overwhelm us. Today, we stand united, stronger than before."

Orion steps forward, his eyes reflecting the early morning light. "The stars align in our favor. My visions have shown a path through the darkness. Together, we can thwart the Conclave's plans."

Valerie, with a confidence that resonates through the room, adds, "The storms are at my command. I'll ensure that no Conclave force can breach our defenses unnoticed."

Samantha, her connection to the natural world ever-present, assures us, "The Earth itself will rise to protect us. I've woven spells that will make Nightshade Mansion an impenetrable fortress."

Lysandra looks up from her notes, her strategic mind meticulously charting our plan of attack. "I've matched each of us with the Conclave member who poses the greatest threat," she says, her gaze sharp. "Orion, your fore-sight will counter Seraphina's illusions. Her mastery of weaving falsehoods into reality can sway the unprepared, but you'll see through her tricks and reveal the truth."

"Valerie," she continues, "your weather control will clash directly with Lucius. He can bend all the elements to his will, but the raw force of your storms can drown out his fire and neutralize his mastery."

"Samantha," she says, pointing directly, "you'll face Isolde. Her shadow manipulation and ability to disappear into darkness are formidable, but your connection with nature will shed light on her hiding places, leaving her no place to conceal herself."

"Laila," Lysandra adds, "you'll handle Malachi. His telepathic reach probes minds and uncovers secrets, but your elemental power and protective magick can create barriers strong enough to deflect his psychic assaults."

"And I," she finishes, her tone unwavering, "will take on their strategist head-on."

The air in the room thickens as we brace ourselves for the battle that will unfold within Nightshade Mansion's grounds. "We defend Nightshade Mansion with everything we've got," she declares, her eyes sweeping across each of us. "When the Conclave shows up, we'll be ready to send them packing."

The room buzzes with a newfound energy, a collective resolve to face the coming storm head-on. As we finalize our plans, the mansion seems to pulse with anticipation, its ancient stones imbued with the magickal defenses we've all contributed to.

The sun crests the horizon, bathing the mansion in golden light as if the dawn itself blesses our endeavor. We step outside, where the air is charged with the power of our united front. Laila raises her arms, calling upon the elements, and a protective barrier forms around the mansion, a shimmering dome of light and energy.

"I've never felt more ready," Saturn says, her voice steady. "For our future, for our child, we will end this threat once and for all."

The group nods, each of us aware of the significance of the coming battle. We are not just fighting for ourselves but for the future of all worlds threatened by the Conclave's darkness.

As we disperse to prepare, I take a moment to absorb the scene before me. Nightshade Mansion stands as a beacon of hope, and its defenders are poised to face the encroaching darkness. Our diverse powers weave a tapestry of protection and strength, each of us harmonizing with the others.

Today, we stand on the precipice of a defining moment in our fight against the Conclave. With our allies beside us and elemental forces at our command, we embrace the dawn's promise—not just as warriors but as a family united in spirit and purpose. We're not just defending the mansion's grounds; we're safeguarding the legacy of Saturn and our unborn child, a symbol of hope and balance for the future.

The eve of battle is upon us, and in the heart of Nightshade Mansion, amidst the swirl of magick and strategy, a quiet confidence takes root. We are ready to reclaim the light, carve a path through the shadow, and secure a future where peace reigns supreme. For the world we're protecting and the child who represents hope, we face this journey together. Our resolve is unbreakable, and our spirits are indomitable. The battle awaits, and we answer its call with unwavering courage, united by a bond that darkness cannot sever.

CHAPTER 20

THE GATHERING STORM

The mansion wakes to gentle morning light spilling through the stained glass, illuminating the kitchen with a spectrum of colors. Despite the turmoil beneath the surface, we all enjoy a relaxed breakfast. Scrambled eggs, flaky croissants, and steaming coffee fill the table as the conversation flows easily, savoring these lighthearted moments before practice begins. Lysandra teases Miles about his addiction to solid coffee while Laila and Samantha swap stories about their latest discoveries in the garden.

"Valerie, how's that storm brewing?" I ask with a grin, knowing she's always got a plan with her weather magick.

"Ready to unleash on the Conclave like a hurricane," she replies with a wink, twirling her fork.

Orion and I dive into a conversation about the moon and its power over the tides. He leans back, gesturing dramatically toward the window. "See, the moon's almost at its zenith. Saturn, you're going to be at full power tonight."

Laughter echoes through the hall as the morning breeze drifts in through the open windows, carrying the scent of blooming flowers. We bask in our camaraderie, sharing jokes and stories. By noon, the lull of morning gives way to a more focused energy as we begin preparing for the battle ahead.

In the afternoon, Lysandra lays out the battle plans, detailing who among us is best suited to face each Conclave member. "They'll be expecting chaos," she says confidently, "but we know who we're up against. We've got this."

We gather our gear and check the moon-tracking app to ensure my power will be fully charged tonight. "It's a full moon," I confirm. "We've got every ounce of magick on our side."

Back in the garden, my haven of calm, I take a moment to breathe in the earthy scent and let the rustling leaves soothe my nerves. Laila joins me, placing a steady hand on my shoulder. "The Conclave thought Julian would be their ace in the hole, but now he's out of play. They won't catch us off guard."

"They're expecting an easy win, but we're ready for them," I reply, gazing up at the familiar mansion walls. "It's my legacy we're defending."

As day surrenders to evening, we gather once more in

the living room, the air buzzing with anticipation and resolve. The mansion, a beacon of light against the encroaching darkness, stands firm with us, its guardians, ready to protect what matters most.

"This battle is for the future," I say, my gaze sweeping across my fellow guardians. "For a world where the next generation can grow up in the light."

The sky above darkens, and the full moon rises, promising victory. Nightshade Mansion becomes a sanctuary of courage, love, and resilience, a lighthouse against the storm. Together, we'll face the coming battle with unwavering resolve, guided by the dawn's promise of triumph.

CHAPTER 21

THE CLASH AT NIGHTSHADE

The full moon casts an eerie silver glow over Nightshade Mansion, illuminating its grounds and heightening the anticipation of the imminent clash. The air is thick with the crackle of magick, and tension radiates like an electric current. Miles stands firmly by my side, offering a reassuring anchor amid the unsettling calm. Lysandra, Valerie, Samantha, Orion, and Laila, embodying elemental strength and ageless wisdom, are poised for battle.

Gathered together under the moon's glow, Lysandra stands at the forefront, scanning our faces as she steels herself for the coming fight. "Okay, you guys, remember who you're matched up with?"

"Seraphina," Orion replies, his gaze unwavering, "I'm ready to expose her illusions."

"Lucius," Valerie declares, her fingers crackling with energy. "I'll drown his fire in a storm."

"Isolde," Samantha says, her voice calm yet firm. "I'll reveal her hiding places and chase her from the shadows."

"Malachi," Laila adds confidently, "I'll block his telepathic reach with everything I've got."

Lysandra nods at each of us, her gaze steady. "Let's protect this place and the people we love."

We fall into position, united in our purpose and ready to send the Conclave packing. The first sign of their arrival is a ripple in the darkness, a disturbance that sets every nerve on edge. "They're here," Miles murmurs, his voice steady as shadows coalesce into recognizable forms at the estate's edge. The air hums with tension, the scent of magick thick and electrifying.

Malachi, a figure of darkness and malevolence, steps forward like a chilling gust against our resolve. "This ends tonight," he sneers, summoning chains of dark energy, his voice dripping with disdain.

Orion boldly steps up, unwavering. "Not while the stars shine upon us." With a sweeping gesture to the sky, he summons a cascade of celestial light that shatters the dark chains before they reach us.

Isolde twists her face with malice and raises spirits from the ground. Laila's chant and a graceful wave of her hand disperse them, returning them to rest. "Your darkness holds no sway here," she declares, her connection to the life force surrounding us shielding us from Isolde's necromancy.

Lucius unleashes a torrent of fire, his eyes ablaze with fury. Valerie steps forward, twisting the air and turning the flames back upon themselves. "Your fire only fuels our determination," she proclaims, her confidence unshaken.

Amidst the chaos, Julian escapes the locked room where he's held. He uses his magick to unravel the enchantments binding him and strides onto the battlefield. "I fight with you," he declares, joining our ranks and turning against his former allies.

Seraphina conjures illusions that mirror our deepest fears, but Samantha calls upon the earth to anchor us in reality. With a decisive sweep of her hand, she dispels the illusions. "Our fears don't define us," she asserts, her connection to the earth shielding us from Seraphina's trickery.

In the midst of it all, Miles finds clarity, his shadow magick guiding him through the melee. He maneuvers through the Conclave's defenses with fluid grace, dismantling their cohesion. "For our future," he whispers, each strike a testament to his resolve.

With the moon at its highest, I raise my hands, and my fingers splayed wide to welcome its ethereal glow. The silvery light bathes me as I draw upon its energy, channeling it to reach across generations. I let the lunar energy infuse me, combining it with the wisdom of my ancestors.

"In the pages of time, old and wise,
    The spirits of kin, a noble prize,
    I call upon my lineage to guide,
    And lend us strength in this fierce tide."

A luminous chain of ancestral spirits appears, their glowing forms encircling us in a shimmering ring. Their presence weaves through the lunar light like intertwined threads, each one a link to my family's legacy.

I continue the spell, my voice reverberating across the battlefield as my ancestors' wisdom guides me.

"To tap the wisdom of those long gone,
    To the ancestral line I draw on.
    By the light of the moon and ancient kin,
    Let this barrier be strong within."

The magick crackles and hums as the spirits encircle us, and a shimmering dome of celestial energy envelops Nightshade Mansion, deflecting the Conclave's assaults. The lunar light mixes with ancestral power, creating a protective barrier that stands firm against Seraphina's illusions, Lucius's flames, Malachi's chains, and Isolde's spirits.

The ancestral spirits channel their wisdom through me, and I let the lunar energy amplify their protection. "Your illusions can't shroud the truth," I call out, weaving through the melee and deflecting each shadow.

"Malachi!" I shout, "You will not break us." The darkness of his chains meets the brightness of my lunar barrier, and his evil energy shatters like glass.

Samantha's roots rise from the ground to ensnare Isolde's specters, while Laila's elemental power shields us from Malachi's psychic assaults. Valerie's storms drive back Lucius, and Orion's foresight exposes Seraphina's illusions. Beside me, Julian defends our family with fierce loyalty, turning against his former allies.

The intensity of the battle escalates as we press our advantage. Orion's celestial beams, Valerie's tempests, Samantha's nature spells, and Laila's life magick converge in a vortex of energy, with Julian's newfound allegiance tipping the scales in our favor.

As the Conclave forces retreat, regrouping under the shroud of night's last embrace, an unexpected turn of events unfolds. Malachi, his gaze cold and unforgiving, locks eyes with Miles and Lysandra. "You were meant to be our greatest assets," he hisses, the venom in his voice palpable. "Yet you chose betrayal, seduced by sentiments and false promises."

Isolde steps forward, her disdain evident. "Falling in love, protecting that witch, and bringing a child into this cursed alliance," she spits out, her words laced with contempt. "Weakness, all of it!"

Lucius, his fists clenched, burns with a rage that

mirrors the fire he commands. "You had a mission, a purpose with the Conclave. But you abandoned it for a fairy tale," he growls, the flames around him dancing in agitation. "Now, you and your precious family will pay the price."

Seraphina joins in with her illusions, sneering. "Love will be your downfall. Your attachment to Saturn and that unborn child has made you vulnerable," she taunts, her illusions growing more vivid, more menacing.

Miles steps forward, his stance resolute, a shield not just in defense of me but of our shared values and the life we've chosen. "Your concept of strength is warped by darkness," he declares, his voice steady despite the threats. "True power lies in the bonds we form, in the love we share, and the future we fight for."

Lysandra, equally undaunted, stands beside Miles, her loyalty unwavering. "We left because we saw through your lies, your vision of a world shrouded in fear and control," she asserts, her eyes blazing with conviction. "We chose a path of light, and if defending our family and our home makes us traitors in your eyes, so be it."

The confrontation reaches a boiling point, the air crackling with magickal energy as we prepare for another round of conflict. But it's Julian's intervention that turns the tide. "Your hate blinds you," he says, addressing his former comrades. "Miles and Lysandra found something worth more than any power you could offer—something you'll never understand because you've never truly felt it."

The Conclave members, fueled by their disdain, launch a desperate assault, a final attempt to eradicate what they cannot comprehend. But we stand united, our love and commitment to each other a fortress impervious to their hatred.

In the final moments of the battle, I hold the prism aloft, its weight heavy with the secrets of ages and the power to control the elements. I feel its energy pulse, knowing it's capable of unimaginable destruction if used by the wrong hands. My voice rings out, steady and unwavering:

"By the light of the stars and the wisdom of the ages,
    This prism of fate shall break their cages.
    Cleanse the chaos that Atlantis once knew,
    Restore the balance to both old and new.
    Let its brilliance cut through their spell,
    And send these dark souls back to where they dwell.
    In its celestial glow, let Earth and Eridanus unite,
    To banish this evil from the world of light."

A radiant column of light erupts from the prism, its power harnessing the elemental forces that the Conclave sought to twist into chaos. The celestial brilliance sweeps through the grounds of Nightshade Mansion, obliterating the Conclave's defenses. Malachi's chains shatter, Isolde's shadows fade, Lucius's flames extinguish, and Seraphina's illusions crumble.

One by one, the Conclave members fall, their bodies vanishing as their dark souls return to Arcturus, the realm where their misdeeds first took root. The prism's light dispels the shadows, restoring elemental balance as dawn's first rays crest the horizon.

The power of the prism settles back into silence, and we stand victorious. The night finally gives way to a new day.

As dawn's light crests the horizon, the grounds of Nightshade Mansion lie serene, a stark contrast to the earlier brutality. The prism's energy settles, and the victorious light shines brightly on the horizon, promising a new day as the world slowly wakes from the darkness.

Victory's quiet settles around us, the air still buzzing with fading echoes of magick and the aftermath of battle. Nightshade Mansion stands resilient, a testament to our defiance, while the dawn heralds new beginnings. We stand, weary but unbowed, ready to face the challenges of the day.

Our hearts, burdened by the weight of our hard-won victory, recognize the enduring cycle of light and darkness. The immediate battle may be over, but the broader war stretches on. We remain vigilant, ready to defend the light whenever darkness looms again.

At this moment, as the rising sun paints the sky with hope, we recognize the strength in our unity, an unbreakable and invincible bond. This hard-earned victory is not just for us but for our future—a future where our child will not only survive but thrive, where the light will not only prevail but illuminate. Nightshade Mansion stands not only to protect but to shine as a beacon of hope in a world liberated from the shadows.

In the aftermath, we gather as a family forged in the crucible of battle. Miles and I, accompanied by our steadfast allies, gaze toward the horizon where the rising sun promises a new beginning. The accusations and hatred from the Conclave of Shadows have not just solidified our bond but fortified it, reinforcing our commitment to each other and the future we are shaping.

"We have shown that love is not a weakness but our greatest strength," I proclaim, my voice resounding with hope. "Together, we will confront whatever challenges lie ahead, for ourselves and for our child."

"We have emerged victorious," Lysandra breathes, her voice tinged with exhaustion and relief. Her face, streaked with dirt and sweat, bears the marks of the battle, but her eyes shine with triumph.

Julian, now among us, appears conflicted yet resolute. "I had never known what it meant to fight for something real until tonight," he confesses, his gaze alternating between mine and Miles's. "Thank you for showing me what true strength is."

Our allies gather around us, their expressions a blend of weariness and triumph. "While this battle may be won, the war continues," Miles declares, his hand finding mine.

Together, we will confront whatever the future holds—for our child, for our world."

The battle fought here, a testament to our resolve and the unbreakable bond that binds us together, shall be remembered not just as a victory over darkness but as a symbol of our unity and love. Our victory is not just for today but for the promise of a brighter future, free from the shadows that seek to engulf us.

CHAPTER 22

THE LEGACY UNFOLDS

It's been four months since we went up against the Conclave of Shadows and won. As the day inches closer to Carina's grand entrance into our world, Miles and I pour our hearts into continuing to transform a spare room into a sanctuary of warmth and dreams. Bathed in gentle hues of pink and blue, the nursery becomes a canvas of our love for her, dotted with plush blankets, an assortment of cuddly toys, each with a story waiting to be told, and tiny clothes arranged with meticulous love. Every item in the room sings a silent promise of joyful moments and the boundless love that's waiting for our little one.

I'm standing there, adding those final loving touches, when a sudden, sharp pain catches me completely off guard. My heart kicks into overdrive, a wild drumbeat of panic and excitement as I realize—it's time. Miles is at my side in an instant, his face a portrait of concern painted with strokes of deep love.

"We've got this, Baby," he says, his voice a rock in the swirling sea of my emotions. He's my unwavering pillar as we navigate our way to the hospital, the roads to UCSF Hospital stretching out like an eternity with every turn and stop amplifying the waves of pain that crash through me.

The hospital envelops us in its efficient, bustling energy, a symphony of professionalism and calm. We're ushered into the labor and delivery unit, a high-tech haven designed to be a cocoon of comfort and safety. Miles is my constant, his encouraging voice a tether holding me to the present. "You're doing amazing, love. Just a little more," he whispers, his hand a comforting weight in mine.

Then, in what feels like both a moment and a lifetime, our daughter announces her arrival with a cry, which is the most beautiful sound I've ever heard. "Here's your baby girl," the doctor says, placing Carina gently in my arms. She's perfect—wavy hair, big hazel eyes mirroring mine, and cheeks just begging to be kissed. Holding her, I'm overwhelmed by a wave of love and wonder. This moment, the culmination of our journey, marks the start of a new chapter filled with love, challenges, and endless possibilities.

Our hospital stay is a blur of sleepless nights and moments so filled with awe, they feel sacred. The room where Carina and I bond in those first days is a quiet sanctuary, a bubble away from the hospital's pulse. It's here, in the quiet lulls between the whirlwind of new parenthood, that the medical staff become our guardians, their expertise and kindness wrapping around us like a warm embrace, making these overwhelming first days a cherished chapter in our story.

Stepping out into the world with Carina nestled in my arms, everything feels different—the city sounds softer, the air seems fresher, and the future glows brighter. Our little family is complete, and as we drive away from UCSF Hospital, I'm filled with a certainty that together, we'll navigate whatever life throws our way, anchored by love, courage, and our unbreakable bond.

Choosing Carina's name was like weaving a dream into reality—it needed to be just perfect. 'Carina' sparkled in our minds like the constellation itself, a beacon of the light and joy she was destined to bring into our lives. Achernar, the constellation's brightest star, symbolizes the resilience and determination I see in her future. And Eridanus, a tribute to our family's legacy, flows through her name like the river it represents, a symbol of the wisdom and strength she inherits.

Holding Carina, I see not just our present but our future in her curious gaze—a future guided by the same stars that have watched over our ancestors. "You're a star seed, Carina," I whisper, promising to teach her about our celestial heritage, about the stars that dance in her name. Her name, Carina Achernar Eridanus, weaves together our hopes, dreams, and the legacy of strong women who've shaped our world. The birthmark on her shoulder, a mirror of the Eridanus constellation, feels like a secret message from the universe itself, a confirmation of our shared destiny. "This mark," I tell her, tracing the pattern, "is our bond, a symbol of the wisdom and strength you inherit."

As dusk settles over Nightshade Mansion, casting long shadows across its grounds, the atmosphere is electric with anticipation. The mansion seems almost alive, its walls whispering secrets of the past and promises of the future.

Miles, ever vigilant, sweeps through the mansion with a practiced eye, his movements a silent testament to his unwavering commitment to our safety. "All clear," he announces, his voice echoing through the grand halls, a beacon of reassurance in the sprawling mansion. Holding Carina close, I whisper promises of the adventures and secrets embedded in the very fabric of this place, "This mansion, my darling, is woven with tales of courage, love, and resilience. You're the newest thread in this rich tapestry."

The November night air is crisp, tinged with the chill of the season as it carries a hint of magick through the grounds of Nightshade Mansion. The grand doors swing open, and the butler steps aside as Aunt Sage strides into the foyer, her swirling cloak trailing behind her. Her eyes, bright with wisdom and strength, meet mine, silently dispelling any lingering doubts. "I've been so excited to see this place," she says warmly, her voice radiating both joy and resolve.

In the living room, Lysandra and Laila stand frozen in disbelief. I rise from my chair, my heart pounding. "Aunt Sage... we thought you were gone," I say, my words catching in my throat.

Lysandra and Laila exchange stunned glances, and then both turn to me with wary expressions. "Is this really your Aunt Sage?" Lysandra asks, her voice tinged with skepticism. "We thought she was dead."

Laila steps forward, her suspicion clear. "After the battle we just won, how can we be sure this isn't an imposter?"

Aunt Sage smiles warmly, her eyes crinkling with a familiar kindness as she looks directly at me. "I understand your concern, my dears, especially after all you've been through. But I assure you, I'm not a trick of the Conclave. Saturn, do you remember the necklace your mother left for you when you were a child? The one she said had protective charms from our ancestors?"

I nod slowly, my breath catching as the memory surfaces. "Yes, I remember."

"Only you and I knew about the inscription hidden inside the clasp," Aunt Sage says, stepping closer. "Check it if you like. I am who I say I am."

Lysandra and Laila exchange another glance before turning to me for reassurance. I nod my heart racing, and move toward Aunt Sage, wrapping her in a tight embrace.

Her familiar warmth washes over me, dispelling any lingering uncertainty.

Lysandra softens, but her tone remains wary. "We'll keep an eye on things, but for now… welcome back, Aunt Sage."

Laila nods, a hint of a smile crossing her lips. "Yes, welcome back."

Aunt Sage turns to them, her gaze steady and filled with kindness. "I understand your concern, but you have nothing to worry about. I'm not here to cause harm. I raised Saturn as my own, and I would never do anything to endanger her or any of you."

We settle into the living room, the soft glow of the crackling fire dancing on the walls. Aunt Sage takes a deep breath, her voice steady and straightforward as she begins her story.

"When I first sensed Daniel's dark intentions, I knew I had to act—not just to protect myself, but to shield Saturn and everyone I cared about," she starts, her words carrying the weight of truth.

"He started coming to my crystal shop, asking about magickal books and showing an unusual interest in rare grimoires. I knew from the start that he wasn't just a curious customer. He kept inquiring about ancient texts, and I had a hunch he was after the family's Book of Shadows. He pretended to be just a mortal, interested in magick after hearing rumors about Saturn's abilities from Dianna."

I lean forward, my voice barely above a whisper. "But what did he do to you?"

Aunt Sage's eyes darken as she continues. "One night, while I was closing up the shop, he showed up with another person. They waited until the street was empty and managed to get me into their car. They took me to a place I didn't recognize, a dark cellar beneath an old building. They thought they could force me to give them the Book of Shadows."

She pauses, her gaze focused and distant as she remembers. "After I realized Daniel wanted the Book of Shadows, it all clicked into place. Years ago, Willow, your mother, and my sister, had warned me about a group called the Conclave of Shadows. She had foreseen that their influence would extend to our family, that their hunger for power would lead them to us."

Aunt Sage's eyes blaze with determination as she continues, "I knew then that Daniel was tied to the Conclave. He was their pawn, and they were using him to access our family's ancient knowledge."

I lean forward, my voice barely above a whisper. "How did you manage to escape?"

Aunt Sage takes a deep breath before speaking. "I knew the spirits of our ancestors would help me if I could channel their guidance. While they interrogated me, I cast a quick charm that made them think I was unconscious. When they left the room to confer with each other, I used the protection spells I had learned from my grandmother to break free of the warded circle."

Her voice grows stronger as she continues. "I slipped out through a basement window, cloaking myself in every protective spell I could muster. I wandered through alleyways until I found a safe place to regroup. The spirits guided me to an abandoned house where I could gather my strength."

She grips my hand tightly, her expression resolute. "I knew that if I disappeared, it would buy you all time to prepare and strengthen your defenses."

The room falls into a hush as her story settles over us like a shroud. Lysandra breaks the silence, her tone filled with admiration. "Your courage saved us all."

Aunt Sage nods slowly, her eyes searching our faces. "It was worth it to see to it that all you are safe, but I've learned that no matter the darkness, we can always find light in each other."

The warmth of the fire and the familiarity of Aunt Sage's presence fill the living room, and for a moment, I feel shielded from the outside world. The darkness beyond Nightshade Mansion can't touch us as we listen to her story, surrounded by family and love.

"With a bit of misdirection and the help of an old friend, I staged my disappearance," Aunt Sage reveals, a hint of mischief flickering in her eyes. "I made Daniel believe he had succeeded, that he had driven me away, all while I stayed hidden, watching his every move, waiting for the right moment to strike back."

The room falls silent, her strategy a testament to her cunning and courage. "And now?" Miles asks, his voice breaking the silence, "What's our next move?"

"We rebuild, we protect, and we prepare," Aunt Sage answers, her gaze sweeping over each of us. "Daniel's defeat doesn't mean the end of our troubles. There are others out there, drawn to your power, your legacy. We must be vigilant."

Her words, though heavy with the promise of future battles, also weave a thread of hope through the fabric of our family's story. "Carina," Aunt Sage turns to me, her expression softening, "Your daughter carries within her the future of our lineage. She is the bridge between the past and the possibilities that lie ahead."

Holding Carina up to Aunt Sage, I feel a surge of pride and determination. "She will know her strength, her heritage, and the power of the love that surrounds her."

Aunt Sage smiles, her eyes reflecting the flickering light of the chandeliers. "Then let us begin," she says, "For the path ahead is long, and it is ours to shape."

As we stand together in Nightshade Mansion, the legacy of our ancestors is a silent witness to our resolve. I feel a deep connection to the past and a hopeful gaze toward the future. Our journey, intertwined with the magick and mystery that pulse through the veins of our home, continues under the watchful gaze of the stars, a testament to the enduring power of love, the strength of our family, and the legacy that we carry forward.

To Be Continued...